THE "MERLIN" SERIES
For Boys and Girls

Twenty-two popular titles by favourite authors
uniform in size and price with this volume

Good Wives	*Louisa M. Alcott*
Jo's Boys	*Louisa M. Alcott*
Little Men	*Louisa M. Alcott*
Little Women	*Louisa M. Alcott*
The Coral Island	*R. M. Ballantyne*
The Dog Crusoe	*R. M. Ballantyne*
The Gorilla Hunters	*R. M. Ballantyne*
Martin Rattler	*R. M. Ballantyne*
The Young Fur Traders	*R. M. Ballantyne*
Alice in Wonderland	*Lewis Carroll*
What Katy Did	*Susan Coolidge*
What Katy Did Next	*Susan Coolidge*
Robinson Crusoe	*Daniel Defoe*
A Perilous Adventure	*Charles Herbert*
Tom Brown's Schooldays	*Thomas Hughes*
Peter the Whaler	*Wm. H. G. Kingston*
Masterman Ready	*Captain Marryat*
The Children of the New Forest	*Captain Marryat*
The Settlers in Canada	*Captain Marryat*
Black Beauty	*Anna Sewell*
Hans Andersen's Fairy Tales	
Robin Hood	

ROBIN HOOD
AND HIS MERRY MEN

AT NOTTINGHAM FAIR

ROBIN HOOD

AND HIS MERRY MEN

Retold by

CHARLES HERBERT

JUVENILE PRODUCTIONS LTD.
LONDON

MADE AND PRINTED IN GREAT BRITAIN BY PURNELL AND SONS, LTD.,
PAULTON (SOMERSET) AND LONDON

E344-644

CONTENTS

ROBIN HOOD
AND HIS MERRY MEN

WHY ROBIN HOOD WENT INTO THE FOREST

"MOTHER! tell me the story of Sir Guy of Coventry, and how he slew the wild blue boar!"

The little ten-year old lad was sitting on a footstool, on the rush-covered floor of the old hall, looking up at the fair lady, clad in a long blue gown, who was his mother.

The dame smiled. "How many times more am I to tell it thee, Robin, lad?"

"It is the only kind of story I care to hear," he declared, as if he meant it. "Except those tales that some of the men who have been with my father to the wars have to tell me of battles."

So in low sweet tones his mother recited to the little lad how Sir Guy of Coventry had gone

out into the forest, single-handed, to attack the
wild blue boar, which had killed several of the
folk as they passed through the forest; and
how he had brought home its grizzly head with
its enormous tusks, and freed the Coventry
folk from their fears. And Robin listened
spell-bound; it was better than a fairy
tale, for "Sir Guy of Coventry" had been
his mother's uncle, and he knew it was a true,
true tale.

The next night there was a huge outcry in
the courtyard of the house, for Robin was missing. He had been missing all the day, but no
one had noticed; for he often went off on his
own, and came back safely enough. But the
night was drawing in, and still Robin had not
come.

The sun had long gone down in the heavens,
and the moon had risen brightly, when, very
tired and very hungry, Robin returned.

"Where hast been?" his mother demanded,
gathering him to her closely, and his father
waited grimly for his answer, whip in hand.

"I did but journey into the forest to see if I
could find a wild boar, and slay him, like ir
Guy!" he answered fearlessly.

"It is fortunate for thee that thou didst not!"

said his father. "But," laying aside his whip, "it was brave of thee to go and try; and hadst thou gone farther into the forest, doubtless, if thou hadst not found a boar, a boar would have found thee."

"There was no boar!" said the boy quietly, and in disappointed tones. "But I fell in with a troop of rough men. They would know how I came thither, and when I told them, they laughed at me," clenching his little fist at the recollection. "But still, they gave me something to eat and to drink, and slapped me on the back, and they said that one day I should, perhaps, find a home in the forest myself."

"May God forbid!" cried his mother; and his father smiled.

"More likely thou wilt become a soldier!" quoth he.

"Ah, but it must be a fine life, this life that those men live, sleeping in the forest, and living in the open air all the livelong day."

This was his first adventure; and after it the years came and the years went, and Robin grew up, little by little coming nearer to manhood. He spent all his time wrestling, leaping and running with the other boys. He learned to fight with the big poles they called quarter-staffs, and with great sticks with handles like a basket, with which they strove to break each other's heads. He learned to be quite at home on the back of a horse, and to set it at high fences, and leap them. But his favourite sport was with his bow and arrows, aiming at a target. So he grew up, a manly, robust young fellow, who could run like a hare, ride like the wind, shoot straight and swift with his bow, and give and take fierce knocks.

His mother noted it. Robin reminded her of her brother, Squire Gamwell, who lived at Great Gamwell Hall, Nottingham, and she felt a sister's craving to show her stout, sturdy son to her brother.

So one day she said to her husband

"My lord, it is some years since I saw my brother, and if it please thee, and thou wilt give me permission, I would well like to journey nigh to Nottingham to see him."

"That will mean that someone must go with thee, mistress. I cannot leave, myself. Who shall I send with thee?"

And she answered, humbly: "If I were to take Robin, he is strong enough to protect me, and though it is a forty-mile ride I shall be safe with him!"

The knight roared with laughter. "Ah!" he said. "Verily I see how it is. The hen wants to show off her stout young chicken. Well, well; it is but natural! Take the lad and go. I shall be glad to know how thy brother fares."

So, a day or two after, dressed in her holiday clothes, Robin's mother came down into the courtyard. Robin was standing there; and he had on his sword, and a dagger in his belt. He sprang lightly into the saddle, and his knightly father lifted up his wife on to the pillion behind Robin, and they began their forty-miles' journey, both on one horse.

So they went along slowly, ambling through the great forest which led towards Nottingham, and for miles they never saw a soul. But when they did once or twice Robin's mother noted with pride how the lad got down and led his horse with his left hand, while his right was ready on the hilt of his sword; for there was no telling whom the stranger might be. The times were stern and rough.

However, they reached Great Gamwell Hall, Nottingham, in safety, and Robin's uncle gladly welcomed Robin's mother; and when he saw the sturdy lad he clapped him on the shoulder, saying: "Verily, we will have some fun, on the morrow, and see what stuff thou art made of!"

So, on the morrow, all the retainers at Gamwell Hall were invited to a feast, at which the young men pitted their strength one against the other; and his uncle insisted that Robin should share their sport. They looked on themselves as very smart and skilled; and with great pride they determined to dress down this young stranger with their quarter-staffs.

But it was their heads which were broken; not his. His quarter-staff whirled about their heads, making quicker play, and when his pole struck theirs, his strength was such that they were driven out of their hands.

"Good!" said his uncle. And he watched him with pride as next he tried to match them with his sword. But it was no match. Robin was quicker on his feet than they, and won in every contest. And the young men of the place began to feel very small.

At last came the trial with the bow and arrows; and here his uncle expected him to be beaten; for the men of the Nottingham district were skilful with the bow. Their arrows went quivering right into the centre of the target. But Robin fixed up a slender rod of willow, and planting it forty paces away, dared them to aim at it.

"What! shoot from such a distance at such a narrow target!" they muttered to one another. "Verily it cannot be done!"

But Robin drew his bow, and taking careful aim, amid the breathless silence of the whole gathering, he shot his arrow, and it split the slender rod in twain. There was a roar of applause and they looked at him with wonder.

After that, while Robin stayed at Gamwell Hall for some time, he became a prime favourite with the Gamwell folk, and their leader in all manner of fun and mischief.

One day he and the Gamwell men went into Nottingham to one of the big fairs. Now, the townsmen looked down upon the men who came in from the villages, and there had never been a fair without there had been a riot. Neither was this fair any happier than the rest. The Gamwell men, feeling insulted by the townsmen, overturned the stalls in the market-place, and the townsmen tried to rush them with their staves, but Robin Hood leapt into the fray, and drove them all before him. Suddenly the townsmen fled in panic, for the Sheriff of Nottingham

had marched his men down to stop the disturb-
ance, and Robin found himself faced with the
officers, who seized him as the ringleader, and
flung him into gaol, on the charge that he had

killed a man whose head he had cracked with
his quarter-staff.

But that night Robin escaped, breaking
through the top of the gaol; and when the
Sheriff heard that he proclaimed that the lad
was to be taken, dead or alive.

Back to Gamwell Hall Robin hurried. He placed his mother upon his horse, carried her back over the forty miles journey by which he had come, and all the way his mind was quiver-

ing with the injustice of the thing. It showed him the times in which he lived; and when at last he reached the old home, and the news reached him that the Sheriff's men were marching to take him, even there he determined he could not mix up his father with his own quarrel with the Sheriff.

"No!" he said. "I will do as so many have done before me. Into the forest I will vanish for a time, and there, in its free, open-air life, I will verily hide myself till the vigour of the hue and cry hath died down." And into the forest he went.

ROBIN HOOD BECOMES A LEADER

"GET me Robin Hood dead or alive!" exclaimed the Sheriff of Nottingham. "What! What! Am I to be bearded in my own town, and that by a mere sturdy lad? Is it to go forth in the county that a man can break out of my common gaol and go scot free? Nay, am I not answerable to the King himself for the taking and the keeping of those who offend the laws and cause a breach of the peace? Get me that Robin Hood, I say, get him—dead or alive!"

When the Sheriff spoke in that way his men knew that they must needs obey. So off they marched to the Hall, where Robin had been staying: but only to be met with sullen looks and the news that the lad had gone back to his own home.

"Forty miles away," quoth their captain. "But if it were sixty ye must foot it bravely!" —which was all very well for him to say. *He* could cheerfully ride ahead; they must follow him afoot.

It was noon next day when they arrived at the house of Robin's father and demanded delivery of Robin in the name of the King's Majesty.

"Ye cannot have him," quoth his father sternly. "He is in the forest, and by this time he is far in! But as ye march through—certes—I should have a care: for they that are on the path that winds through the glades make excellent marks for the arrows of men who are skilled with the bow. Perchance some of ye will never see Nottingham again!"

The Sheriff's men insisted upon searching house and grounds just to prove Robin was not there. Then they departed, baffled, and marched off in the direction of the forest; but when they reached the spot at which the path led through glades, where hidden marksmen might lurk with ease, they thought better of it and decided to take the winding road to Nottingham, though it was longer!

Meanwhile, how was it with Robin?

He had entered the forest in the evening time, and wandering through the lonely glades, he cast himself down to think. Presently, as the night grew chilly, he gathered some heaps of leaves and brushwood; then, with his flint and steel, he gained a spark and let it fall upon a piece of tinder-wool which he had in his box. Then he placed the smouldering tinder on the heap of dried leaves and blew it into a flame, and very quickly had a bright fire burning.

But his movements had been watched! The distant glow of his fire had been marked, and outlaws like himself, but who had been there a long time, stealthily gathered around him, ever creeping closer and closer. They saw him wrap himself in his cloak and cast himself down to slumber; and no sooner did he seem off guard than they rushed at him; and he stirred to find himself surrounded by rough men who were demanding to know who he was and why he was there.

"I am here for but one reason," quoth Robin. "There is in Nottingham a man known as 'the Sheriff'—ah! methinks ye have heard of him!" —this as he saw them laugh. "That Sheriff invited me to be his guest; in very sooth he would take no refusal. He paid me such very pressing attentions that verily I had to go. But the same night I was missing, and sin' then he hath been very eager to see me—so eager, indeed, that he careth little whether it be alive or dead. Alive he shall never take me, and as I have no intention at present of dying, I just changed my address. That is why I came. And if ye would further know what I came for, then I tell ye, 'I have come To Stay.'"

So they let him stay, satisfied he was no spy upon their movements; and they invited him to make common cause with them and take his food with them. "If ever," they said, "ye shall happen to want food, we live on the King's deer and the venison from it, and there are birds in the trees which can also be shot and cooked."

So Robin joined them.

That was how Robin found himself one of a band. But there was another reason. The story of his escape was gossiped about in a great many villages around that side of the forest where his father's home was. It was also gossiped about in the villages on that side of the forest where his uncle's home was, at Gamwell Hall. They remembered the lively youngster who had come amongst them only a little time and shown them how wonderfully he could use his quarter-staff, his sword, and, above all, his bow and arrows.

So when anything went wrong with any of these villagers, he said to himself: "I will now go and join myself to Robin Hood."

One after another came, and presently there were so many who were attracted by the presence of Robin Hood that the outlaws who were there before felt that Robin must be rather an important man, a man of much higher rank than themselves.

So he was! On his mother's side he would have been very likely, on the death of just one or two men, to have become the Earl of Huntingdon, while on his father's side he was related to a very knightly and noble family.

It was quite natural that Robin Hood, of such good family, especially one who could so use his fists, and his good staff, and his sword, and his bow and arrows, should after a bit begin to be looked upon as a leader. And when the others who came after Robin came because they were attracted by his being there, then it was only a little time before he became chief by common consent.

Bit by bit the band grew until it numbered

140 archers, who were wonderfully skilled, and Robin took care to keep them all in constant practice. Once he became their leader he insisted that they should only get the very best of bows, made of strong, pliable yew. The shafts of their bows—that is, the arrows—were exactly a yard long. The arrows were broad, or pricked to a point, or were made round. They also wore short swords.

One night, as they sat around the camp fires, he said to them:

"Would it not be wise if we all dressed ourselves in green cloth?" And as they listened, wondering wherefore, he went on: "I mean that as the trees are green, any of us who are wearing the same colour will in good sooth be less likely to be noticed." And they thought it one of the cleverest and finest ideas, and they did as he said.

Another night he began to play upon a bugle, and showed them how they could talk upon it. How running up the scale of notes fast could be made to mean a cry for help; how, if they sounded two notes together quickly, they could know it was someone calling; and how, if it were only one sharp blast, they might know it was himself. "Do ye agree amongst yourselves as to what notes shall stand for your leaders?" And they did. For there were leaders, because Robin had divided

his 140 men into bands, each of which had a leader.

So here he was, chief of a band of men, and the more he looked at them the more he racked his brains to know what was the best thing he could give them to do.

Little by little a plan formed in his head, and
a daring plan it was! The first thing he determined to do was to get the very best men from
the villages round to join his ranks. If he heard

of a very tall, or a very strong man, or one
who was very skilled in wrestling and fighting,
he would go down to that village disguised
like a beggar or a tramp. Then he would
get to know them better, and presently have

a pretended quarrel with them. When he had tried out what they could do by making them fight with him, he would tell them who he was, and ask them to join in with him and his Merry Men. So at last he gathered together a splendid band of men, about whom people began to talk far and wide.

Then, little by little, he began to tell them his plans.

"Verily," he said to them, "we shall be little better than fools if we skulk here as if we were villains. This is no part for me nor for you to play. Listen," he cried, "we are living in strange times. There seemeth one set of rules for the poor and another for the rich. And I say it isn't fair! The sheriffs look after the poor, but dare not touch the rich. Let us look after the sheriffs! The barons in their castles do as they like. Let us look after the barons!"

His men roared with laughter.

"Why laugh?" he went on. "There are 140 of us—as good men as ever drew an arrow, either at a venture or a target. And outside the forest are a good many targets. Bad men, bad things, bad ways. Let's go and alter them!

" Yes, the men who 'right the wrong' will be Robin Hood and yourselves. D'ye pledge me your word to it?"

And with uplifted hand they swore "to right the wrong!"

HOW LITTLE JOHN JOINED THE BAND

ROBIN HOOD was feeling rather dull: in fact he had a fit of the "blues." It is all very well to be the leader of a band of hefty men; but his band of outlaws was growing larger and larger. It was a fine set of men; but what is the use of a magnificent machine unless you can give it something to do? They had had no real adventure and no sport for fourteen long days. So Robin Hood said to himself:

"It is no good waiting here in the forest for some adventure to come along. It is getting deadly dull here. I must go outside the forest and seek for something more stirring."

So it came to pass that he left his Merry Men to come out behind him, and threaded his way through the dense undergrowth of the forest, and presently, after much patient walking, he emerged into one of the country roads.

Just as if he were a mere countryman passing from one place to another he lumbered along aimlessly, until presently he came to a path across the fields which led up to a distant village, and decided to wend his way in that direction.

He had not been long walking before he came to a part of the field where the path ended at a rude wooden bridge, made of planks, over which anyone must cross if they wished to get into the field beyond; for the bridge was placed over a stream, which ran and gurgled merrily beneath.

There was no difficulty about getting on to the bridge; but no sooner had Robin Hood stepped upon it, than he saw the difficulty would be to get off, for there, at the other end of the plank footway, loitered a burly stranger. He was leaning against the rude oak hand-rail which had been put up by the folk who had made the bridge, and he looked at Robin Hood insolently, but never made the least attempt to allow Robin to pass.

Now when two obstinate goats meet on a narrow mountain pass where there is only room for one, it stands to reason that one of them must go back, or one of them must lie down and let the other step over him, or else they must fight it out, and which ever manages to fling the other over the mountain-side will be victorious. This stranger and Robin Hood were like those two mountain goats.

It was quite evident that the stranger did not intend to move; it was equally clear from the way Robin Hood came on, that he intended to pass. So they stood and simply glared at one another.

Said Robin Hood, "Fellow, let me pass!" But the huge seven-foot-high loiterer never budged.

Said Robin Hood, "If you don't move out of my way, you great oaf, I shall have to move thee!" But the great oaf only grinned.

Then Robin Hood unslung his bow, and was about to fit an arrow to it, saying, "If you don't move I'll show you how we Nottingham men can use the swift-winged arrow!"

But the other lumbered forward, raising his quarter-staff, and said grimly, "If you but touch the string with your shaft, I'll dust your hide for you; in fact I won't wait for you to do it!" And he was advancing upon Robin swiftly, but Robin backed slightly, and as he moved fitted the arrow on to the string, and the two stood there threatening each other; and, had he but known it, that seven-foot stranger was nearer to death that moment than he had ever been. At last Robin said:

"Thine is but foolish talk! I can send a dart through thy heart in quicker time than it takes to tell it!" And he covered the stranger with his bow. But the stranger exclaimed, scornfully:

"Thou art but a coward! Thou art armed with bow and arrows. I only have my stout staff!"

Said Robin Hood: "'Coward!' I like that! I'll soon prove to thee I am no 'coward.' Wait here but a minute or two, and I'll make me a staff: then, staff to staff, and foot to foot, we'll fight it out!" And he stepped off the bridge, and going to a near-by oak sprang at one of the branches, and by sheer force bent it down, and wrenched it from its hold. Then he tore it off, and stripping it of twigs, he was back in a few minutes, running at the stranger with his ready-made weapon.

They met in the middle of the slight bridge, and flourished their staves, and Robin got in a bang on the side of the stranger which made his very bones ring. But while he was doing it the stranger cracked him on the head. Robin reeled, but, pulling himself together, he rained

in a shower of thick and fast blows, till, suddenly,
the tall stranger, who had the advantage of a
long reach, gave him one blow which made
him stagger, and then suddenly used the other
end of his staff to tumble Robin off his foothold
and he fell into the brook beneath.

"Ah, where are you now, my fine fellow?"
grinned the stranger.

There had been heavy rains, and the brook
was swollen, and it was fairly deep: so Robin
replied, as he spluttered with the water he had
gulped in his fall:

"I'm in the flood and floating along with
the tide! You've proved yourself the best
man. I own I'm beaten, and the fight's at an
end."

"All right!" said the other. "So long as you
own you're beaten I'll let you cross the bridge
when you can get out."

So Robin waded out, lower down the stream,
muddy and wet, and came back and began to
talk to the stranger. He asked him if he had
anything to do, and the stranger declared that
he had not.

"There's no one within miles will give John
Little"—and he tapped himself as he spoke—
"even a day's work. They're all afraid of me!

I work my own way and they want me to work theirs. Masters and men—they're all alike and try to make me go their way. But no one ever made John Little do anything, and they get broken heads, and I have to wander on hungry. I want a good meal now!" And he rubbed his stomach.

"All right!" said Robin. "You come back with me and I'll show you a band of good fellows who'll be glad to feed you!" And he turned back the way he came, the stranger lumbering his huge body along with him. But when they entered Sherwood Forest, Robin blew his horn, for he knew that his men would follow him at a distance, as they generally did, in case of trouble, and he expected they were somewhere about.

He was right! In a minute or two other horns answered his call, and seventy-nine bowmen, clad in Lincoln green, surrounded them, and came up to their chief.

Robin Hood gazed at them proudly. "These be my Merry Men, O John Little! And this" —turning to his men—"is a man who would not let me pass across a bridge this morn, and tumbled me into a stream. What shall we do with him?"

"Duck him," they cried. "Serve him the same, the silly varlet!"

But Robin would not let them. "No," he said. "He has proved himself a wonder with his staff. He had far better join us. Wilt join us?" he queried. "We have plenty to eat and to drink, and as for the work we have to do —well, our work is to 'Right the Wrong'! If there is a tyrant anywhere about!—if anyone is mean to his neighbours!—if a man robs the poor!—he has to settle with us. There is plenty of fighting: a hard life, and fine sport. Wilt throw in thy lot with us, John Little?"

John Little said he would. And he went back with them to their camp, and, when they reached it, Robin Hood said to his Merry Men, winking at them mischievously:

"You will have to re-christen him!" So they roared with laughter, and, swarming round John Little, they dragged him on to the ground and poured over him mugsful of beer; and when they cudgelled their brains for a new name to give him, one of them, called Will Scarlett, exclaimed:

"He says he's 'John Little'; let's call him 'Little John' because he isn't."

So John Little became 'Little John' from that day forward. They dressed him in their uniform of Lincoln green. He stayed with them many days and they taught him to shoot, and to

use the sword and the dagger, and he shared in the life of Robin Hood and his Merry Men. He never knew again what it was to be hungry; for had they not the deer of the forest and the birds of the trees to eat? If Little John was quarrelsome, he was amongst men who understood that and gave him plenty of chances to let his quarrelsomeness show in the right cause.

He fought his way into their favour bit by

bit. Even the stoutest amongst them met his match when this great giant began to lay about him with his quarter-staff; and as he showed unfailing good temper, so long as none of them professed to believe he could beat him, he quickly became a prime favourite with them all, so much so that, when Robin Hood went off by himself, he even left Little John in charge of them all, and the Merry Men loved to have it so.

THE RULES OF THE GAME

"Who tied this man's hands behind him in this ruthless fashion?" demanded Robin Hood, turning upon his men full of wrath.

They had suddenly surrounded a Packman as he wended his way along the forest path, and brought him and the bundles packed upon his horse back to the clearing.

They looked at one another in surprise. Then Little John, the seven-foot giant, up spoke and said: "I did it! Is't not well done? Methought I trussed him up in right good fashion."

"Thou didst!" quoth Robin. "Verily, thou didst! Here," turning to the rest of them, "seize you, for me, Little John, and truss him up in the same way!" And, despite the struggles of the giant, his hands were brought behind his back, and tied, even as he had tied the hands of the Packman, so that his bonds cut into his wrist. But though they did the will

of their chief, there were black looks amongst
them all, as if they did it unwillingly.

Robin noted it, but, none the less, he turned
to Little John, and said: "Now, how likest
it thyself? Could ye not have tied his hands

more loosely? Is't not bad enough to be taken
captive without making the taking a harder
thing for them? Tie not too tight! Or verily,
I will tie ye! Handle not too roughly, or in
very sooth I will have ye no more remain men

of my troop. Men of strong arms and brawny
shoulders do I want, but behind them I want
men of gentle hearts. If ye have not both
ye are not the men for me. You have had
your lesson, and now untie Little John. Little
John, I know you well enough, and ye know
me well enough, not to mind my rough usage.
I did it but to show the rest my will concerning
all whom ye take."

Little John, when the thongs were removed,
looked ruefully at his wrists, and said to the
prisoner: "In good sooth I knew not I had
tied thee so tight. It was, even as our chief
has said, galling enough to be dragged here
at all without scarring thy wrists."

"Right handsomely said!" quoth Robin.
"And now," turning to the captive Packman,
"sit ye down on the green sward and tell us
whither thou didst carry thy goods, and whence
thou hast come!"

"It was but this morn, as the sun rose in
the heavens, that I set out from Nottingham
with these goods. Thou seest I am but a young
man. I have not long been engaged in business.
In Nottingham I found it was slow work waiting
for customers to come to me. So I said to myself: 'Pack thou thy steed with some of thy

coarser cloth, and get thee to the villages. It may be there are yeomen and their wives, and labourers and their women, who will gladly buy a yard or two from thee.' Even so I did. But as I wandered along the path thy men surprised me and brought me hither. I am grieved at heart that I knew not I should fall into the company of such a host; for verily, I would have brought with me some cloth of Lincoln green to sell ye. There is nought in my pack that will be of service to any one of you. There are russet-browns, and greys, and drab, but there is not a yard of Lincoln green."

Robin and his Merry Men burst out laughing. The way in which this man seemed to take it for granted that he had missed a bargain tickled them to death.

"Then ye were not journeying to sell some fine dainty stuffs to the squires of the district and their ladies?" queried Robin.

"Nay," quoth the man. "Had I done so they might have helped themselves, and left me to collect my moneys how I could. For we live in a time, my masters, when Might is Right."

Robin nodded, as if he agreed with him, and said to his men:

"Open his pack, and, if he has spoken the truth, and was but journeying to sell to honest poor folk, verily, he shall go on his way unmolested."

They found it even so as the Packman had said. There were bales of russet-browns, and cloth of grey and drab, such as common folk would wear; and there was stout holland for their aprons, but never a yard that knight or dame, or squire or lady, would have dreamed of wearing.

"The man has spoken truth!" declared Robin. "And, inasmuch as we war not upon the poor, and would not we should interfere with their chance of buying some new smock and jackets, methinks my men would rather let you go your way. Is't not so?" turning to his men.

The men broke out into loud applause, and the Packman breathed freely.

"Verily, I will ride this way again," quoth he. "And when I do I will bring with me some bales of Lincoln green. In good sooth, methinks I ought to do a good trade with ye, for there are at least a hundred of ye."

"You are sure, then, that we would pay thee for thy goods?" said Little John.

"So sure, that it will not be long before ye shall see me again."

After Robin had given him a good meal of venison and ale, the Packman went to the villages, and there he told them how well Robin had treated him, and wherefore he had spared him. So they knew that Robin and his Merry Men were their friends. But the men of Robin's band took home the lesson from that day— that they were to treat their captives gently, and that they were not to disturb the interests of the common folk.

The Packman was as good as his word. Scarce a week went by when he returned, and on the back of his good mare he carried some cloth of Lincoln green, which he sold to the outlaws, and even as he had thought so it came to pass; for they paid him in full for what he sold them. But a week later he came back, and there was trouble writ all over his countenance, and the story he had to tell was this:

"After I left ye all, methinks I must have gone astray near Nottingham, for in the dusk I must have left the bridle path. And, even as I wandered round, I was set upon by another band of robbers, who took my money and my nag, and left me there to find my way home as I would."

"Lead us to the place where thou didst go wrong!" demanded Robin, and somewhat unwillingly the man did set out.

"Methinks it was here that I wandered off the bridle path!" he declared. But search as Robin and his Merry Men would, there were no marks that a beast had done otherwise than go straight forward. Neither were there any marks of a struggle. Robin noted it, and in obedience to his orders they marched the Packman back to the camp, while two of Robin's men were despatched, unknown to the Packman, to his house and shop in the town.

"Thou must abide as our guest until to-morrow even," quoth Robin, "while we try to find with whom thy goods went astray." And even as Robin spoke, he saw the man looked uncomfortable.

It was the next afternoon before Robin's messengers returned, and as they appeared out of the forest in the clearing, Robin, who was expecting them, went forward to meet them.

"The man has lied!" they said. "For we found the nag which he says was stolen, there in his stable!"

Then, in a fury, Robin strode to the Packman and said: "Thou art verily a good trader. Thou didst think to thyself, 'Verily Robin Hood and his Merry Men are good of heart.

I will go and return to them, and tell them I have been robbed; and it may be they will give me money to help me.' It was thy bad fortune that thou didst say they had also stolen thy nag, for my men have found thy nag at home in thy stable. Therefore this is my sentence."

The Merry Men of Robin Hood listened eagerly.

"This is my sentence," quoth Robin. "Thou Ananias! For money thou didst lie, and with money thou shalt pay. Here ye shall bide, until, at thy request, someone from thy home shall bring thee a ransom. Every penny thou didst make from us thou shalt return, but only thy profits. We would not stoop to rob thee of a penny." And as he said, so it was.

Then the justice that ruled in the mind of Robin Hood began to dawn upon his Merry Men. They began to understand that it was in Robin's mind to hurt no ploughman, no yeoman, and not even any knight or squire who were good fellows. But if they knew of anyone cheating, and robbing, and lying, they were to look on themselves as instruments of justice on such men. If any of their captives said they had no money, and they found some, then, because of their lie, they should take a double gift.

They talked these things over with Robin, and he established these things as the rules of the game.

"Help the good yeomen, and they that already find life difficult!" quoth he. "But as for them who make it so, they are our enemies, and we are theirs, especially the Sheriff of Nottingham!"

And they said, "We will keep thy word and obey it!"

ROBIN HOOD AND WILL SCARLETT

ROBIN HOOD was a very changeable kind of man. One day he was full of fun and practical jokes, the life and soul of all his Merry Men; another, perhaps even the next day, he was irritable and fidgety. On some days he would scarcely speak to a soul, and would sit about thinking, thinking, thinking! Presently he would spring to his feet, and with a brief, "You men will see me when you see me," he would wander off.

To-day was one of these days! Nearly all the week through he had scarcely spoken a word: and it had finished up by his suddenly breaking away from them all, and vanishing into the forest. His men knew him, and his moods, too well to think of questioning him. They simply let him go!

Robin wandered off into the greenwood. He had learnt by experience that the best way to shake off a wretched mood like this was to go for a long, long tramp. The beautiful greenery of the interlacing trees seemed to soothe his troubled spirit, and the walk seemed to shake off the homesickness which he felt. Yes, "home-sickness": for, though it was a glorious and carefree life, this life which he lived with his Merry Men, there were times when he would have given a great deal to be back in his father's home and to see his mother again. He loved the comradeship of his Merry Men: but no one can exactly take the place of one's family! It was this feeling which had led Robin Hood into his present mood, and as he tramped along through the forest glades, it was this mood he was trying to get the better of.

An hour or two later he had reached the edge of the forest along the Nottingham road, and suddenly he caught sight of a young man who evidently belonged to some good family. His doublet was all silk: his stockings were scarlet in hue, and, standing on the edge of the green carpet of the forest, he made a bright spot of ruddy colour.

"I wonder what he is doing!" murmured Robin to himself. "He is clearly watching that herd of deer!" For near at hand there was a fine company of the King's deer browsing.

Robin Hood drew closer to him, and presently he distinctly heard him say, just as though he were speaking to the deer:—

"I will have the best of you for my meal to-day, and very quickly too!"—and to Robin's astonishment—for he knew that everyone else knew how it was forbidden to kill one of the King's deer—to Robin's astonishment he saw this strange-looking young man fit an arrow to his bow, and take steady aim.

He was quite forty yards away from the nearest wanderer from the herd, but, in spite of that distance, the young man's arrow sped straight to its mark, and the wounded deer dropped where it stood, shot through the heart, while the rest scampered away in panic.

All this time Robin Hood had been quietly observing him, and now he cried, loudly, "Well done! Well hit!"

The young man in the scarlet stockings jumped in dismay. He was startled, and at first he thought that Robin was one of the foresters of the place and, if so, he knew that he had been caught red-handed in a crime, which was sufficient to hang a man, and he had no wish to feel the noose around his neck. Not he!

So, acting upon this idea, he felt it was better to be the attacking party instead of waiting to be attacked; so he cried to Robin:

"A second shot can be as good: and if you don't clear off, this will find a target in your ribs." But Robin never moved, although the other was covering him with his weapon. He never budged an inch.

So they stood facing one another, and presently Robin said: "I say again, 'Well done!'—Why, to bring down that deer at forty yards means no slight marksman!"

Suddenly, the young man dropped his bow and made towards Robin with raised fists, exclaiming: "And if thou dost not take thy carcase out of the way, and that right quickly, then I will dress thee down for thy pains. What is't to thee whether I kill one of the deer or no? Answer me that?"

"Hoity-toity," mocked Robin. "If thou art so put out with a man who did but pay thee a well-deserved compliment, what kind of wild beast wouldst thou be to one who miscalled thee?"

"Drop thy banter and fight me!" exclaimed the other.

"Oh, young man, I am willing enough to fight. I love fighting for its own sake; but, for what should I fight thee? I do not fight with every ill-tempered varlet who crosses my path. When I fight it is with a lad of finer mettle than thou art."

"Boasts, mere boasts!" returned the other; rushing to his bow to once more draw upon Robin, but as he turned he found that Robin was already covering him with his own ready-drawn weapon.

"Now," cried Robin, "move but a step and I send this flying towards thyself! But if thou wishest to fight, then thou hast a sword by thy side, and so have I. Thou art clearly the son of a good house and hast a right to wear a sword. So unsheathe thy blade and I will cross swords with thee!"

No sooner said than it was done! The stranger drew his blade and very quickly there came a clashing of swords as steel met steel. But they had not been long fighting before Robin found, to his surprise, that the young man was a fine swordsman, and he had hard work to hold his own. . . . Practised as Robin was in every feint and pass and thrust, he discovered that the young man was ready for him and that he must fence right carefully or he would have his own defences broken through.

But as they fought on breathlessly, Robin was thinking hard. "Oh," he wondered, "if only I could induce this young man to join my band. He would be the very thing for us. . . ." So he pressed him hard, and presently he began to see that the stranger was losing his breath, and that if he only attacked him harder he would have him at his mercy. So he made for him feverishly and it was not long before the stranger gave back.

At last they paused for a minute's breathing space. And then Robin said, quietly: "Listen to me! Thou art a stout lad, whoever thou art. Hast a mind for a life of venture?"

"'Mind,' for it," quoth the other. "In very deed that is why I am here at all. I am seeking to join the band of Robin Hood."

"Oh, art thou? And wherefore to join his band? Knowest thou not he is an outlaw and every man's hand against him?"

"He is my cousin," said the young man.

"Thy cousin? Then who art thou, and what is thy name?"

"My name is Gamwell, and I come from Gamwell Hall. Robin, my cousin, paid us a

visit sometime back and my mind was drawn
to him. He . . . why, now I come to think
of it . . . he was something like thee in
appearance."

"I am HE," remarked Robin quietly. "I
have been hungering for a sight of my own
kith and kin, and lo, this very day it seems
that one of them has been seeking me!" And
he dropped his sword into its sheath, saying:

"Thou must be my Cousin Will: and thou art welcome to me as the flowers in May. I must take thee to my Merry Men, but as we go thou shalt tell me why thou dost feel impelled to leave thy father's house at Gamwell Hall and cast in thy lot with us. What hast thou done?"

"Verily I had an accident, in which I nearly killed one of my father's stewards. The man may live, but then, on the other hand, he may die; so I took time by the forelock and, as I have often wanted to join thee in thy life of which I have heard ever since thou didst flee the Sheriff of Nottingham, I have come here this day."

"And so thou shalt," quoth Robin. "So thou shalt! I will lead thee to the men, and they will make thee as one of ourselves; only they will want to baptise thee first!" And his eyes twinkled as he spoke; for he had thought of a fine new name for his young cousin.

After walking for some time they came to a glade, where Robin blew the well-known call upon his horn, and the men came running, and were astonished to see their chief with this young stranger; but when he told them who he was and wherefore he was there then they made him welcome gladly for Robin

Hood's sake. There was no need for him to
eat of the deer which he had killed for they
made him partake of their meal, and made a
special feast of it for his sake in token of their

welcome; but, as Robin had foreseen, they
wanted to christen him afresh, in their usual
boisterous way, and when they ransacked their
brains for a new name for him it was Robin,
himself, who found it for them.

"Look at his stockings!" he said. "Finer scarlet never graced a young man's leg. Scarlet they are in very deed, and Will is his name: so 'Will Scarlett' shall he be called."

So that was how Will Scarlett came to join the band, and that was how he got his name.

ROBIN HOOD AND THE POOR KNIGHT

ROBIN HOOD had another of his strange moods upon him. He loved change. The folk whom his Merry Men brought in prisoners from time to time had no idea how welcome their presence was to Robin. Even if they had been able to pay no ransom; even if there were no goods in their pack, still he would have been glad to see them, for they made someone to talk to. They brought some news of the outside world; and even to see them and listen to them was change. Robin was very fond of all his Merry Men, especially of Will Scarlett and Little John: but one can have too much even of a good thing.

Many days had gone by since any strange guest had sat down to a meal with them in their forest home; and Robin was feeling bored as he sat there mending bows and arrows. Dinner time came, and those who had been cooking the meal told Robin it was ready.

But Robin did not come, and at last he said,
"See ye here! I am not going to eat, nor give
the sign for you to begin, until you have brought
in some guest to share our meal with us."

The men looked at one another! They did
not attempt to argue with him; they knew
Robin too well: knew that he was as obstinate
and self-willed as a spoilt child; but he had so
many good qualities that they loved him in
spite of his faults, so just to humour him,
Little John, Will Scarlett and another man
set off to find a guest.

Now it fell upon that day that a certain
knight, named Sir Richard of Lea, who was
journeying to a neighbouring abbey, came
riding by through the forest path which led to
the lands around Nottingham. His very name
showed he really was a knight, but there was
very little else about him to show it. Most
of the knights of that time looked like knights.
Their chain armour was polished and bright.
Their surcoats were of rich material, and the
coverings of their horses made of costly fancy
stuffs. But this knight was shabby from head
to foot, and so was his horse.

As Little John and Will Scarlett and their
companion caught sight of him ambling along,

Sir Richard looked such a sorry specimen that he scarcely seemed worth stopping. However, he was the first man met; and as they had not gone far, and were in a hurry to get back to dinner, they stopped him, and Little John cried:

"Welcome, Sir Stranger! May we invite you to turn aside and eat a meal with our master?"

"Who is your master?"

And when they answered, "It is Robin Hood!" he replied, "Ah, I have heard much that is good of him, and I shall be pleased to have the chance of saying afterwards that I have met him."

So they took him along with them to the camp. There he dismounted, and the Merry Men, as if they were his servants, waited upon him; led him to the brook where he could lave his hands and face, and refresh himself by bathing his feet, and then they all sat down to dinner.

At least, they were about to, but the strange knight looked at the well-spread table of boards on which were placed all manner of smoking birds, great pieces of beef, and great haunches of venison, and several pasties, and he seemed strangely reluctant. Indeed, he at once very

c

politely remarked to Robin Hood: "Verily, I have not seen a meal like this for many a long day; and since I cannot pay for it at all, I do not think it right that I should sit down with ye."

"Tell me the truth," quoth Robin, looking the knight straight in the face. "Tell me on the honour of a knight how much money hast thou with thee?"

"By my knightly honour I have no more than ten shillings!"

"Then," said Robin cheerfully, "the meal shall not cost thee one penny! Sit down, man." But while they began to dine he whispered to Little John to go and see whether in the pockets of the traveller's cloak there was more than he had said. But Little John returned, saying that it was even so.

They fell to feasting, and presently Robin inquired, after the knight had eaten and drunk well: "Tell me, my knightly guest, how it has come to pass that thou art in this plight?"

"It is the result of misfortune!" said the knight. "I have done nothing wrong. My ancestors were men of substance. It is not long since I could swagger it with the best, and now I have nothing!" His face filled with gloom, and his voice trembled. So Robin waited a moment, and then he asked why, and how.

"My son was engaged in a tournament, and by chance in the tourney he pierced a knight's helmet by accident. It was decreed, after the

knight died, that he should pay a large fine. So, to save him from prison, I borrowed the money from the Abbot of St. Mary's, promising that if I did not pay it back on a certain day I would hand over to him all my lands, which are worth ever so much more. That day is to-morrow; so, as I cannot pay, I am going to the abbey to give up my lands."

Robin Hood questioned him as to how much he owed, and when he heard that it was £400, a very big sum in those days, he asked him why he did not borrow it from someone else. But the knight answered: "Who would lend a broken-down man such a sum of money, which I should have to admit that I only wanted because I could not already pay it."

Robin Hood thought deeply for a moment or two, and then he said:

"There is about thee that that I like! In very deed, I believe thy story. It is a misfortune that verily might have overtaken the most careful of men. Thou must be a good father to have taken upon thee the burden of thy son's troubles in this fashion. Go thou to the abbey, and on the morrow, when the money is due, do thou beg of the Abbot to give thee a longer time in which to pay. But, an' if he will not listen, and from what I have heard of the Abbot, he is already licking his lips at the thought of getting such fine lands into his own hands and, therefore, will not grant thee time, then do thou disappoint him by paying him the money in full!—I should like to be there to see the sourness of his face when thou dost produce it."

"Verily, it would be a good joke!" laughed the knight, "but where could I produce it from?"

"I will lend it thee," said Robin sturdily.

"And I will trust thee to repay it when thou canst. Little John! Do thou go to the treasury and bring forth £400 and give it unto this knight."

Little John went to the place in which they kept the money which had come to them, some of it from ransom which had been paid them, and much of it from money which had been given them as wages by the farmers and squires of the neighbourhood to protect them from other robber bands. Oh, there were piles and piles of it, which had grown: for the simple reason they had so little to spend it on, since their food cost them nothing and their forest lodgings were rent-free.

Little John brought back the £400, and then Robin said:

"Thou must not go to this Abbot looking as if this £400 were all thou dost possess in the world. Thou shalt look, yea, verily, thou shalt look as though thou art a lucky, prosperous knight."

So he had the knight armed with goodly armour from his head even to the spurs upon his heels. He covered him with a surtout of cloth of gold. He gave him a fine horse, beautifully caparisoned with rich tapestry, and harnessed with silver harness; and for the first time for many weary months, Sir Richard of Lea felt that he looked like a knight who could hold up his head with the highest in the land. Well fed, well clothed, well armed, well mounted, it was a different man who stood before their

delighted eyes; for all the Merry Men had
caught the infection of his kindness from
Robin, and entered into the spirit of the
thing.

Robin shook the stranger's hand heartily
in a farewell grip, and wished him "God
speed!"

"If the Abbot accepts the money before
witnesses, thou canst ride away a happier
man!" quoth Robin. "But from what I have
heard, he and his monks may even yet play
thee a scurvy trick, so I and my men will
watch out for thy return this way. An', if thou
comest not, we will make enquiries as to thy
welfare. But, if it should come to pass that all
goeth well with thee—as it may—for the
Abbot may be better than report painteth him,
it will be as well, before thou ridest away now,
if thou dost pledge thyself, in the presence of
these Merry Men of mine, what time thou
wilt return unto us and pay us back some of
the £400 we have entrusted thee."

Sir Richard of Lea thought earnestly for a
little time, and then said:

"In the presence of these Merry Men of thine,
by my knightly honour, I pledge myself to
return hither, and pay back as much of this

money as I can gather, and all of it, if it be possible, ONE YEAR FROM THIS DAY!"

So Sir Richard of Lea rode away towards the Abbot of St. Mary's, and, verily, if the rest of him were as light as his heart, his good steed felt no weight.

THE KNIGHT AND THE ABBOT

THE Abbot of St. Mary's was sitting in his own special room, and, as it was just after breakfast, the expression on his face was that of a man who had well dined. But that was not the reason for his pleasant looks! He had something better in his mind than the mere memory of a good meal: yes, a far sweeter recollection still! Why, that very morning, when he had awaked, the first thought that had come to him was this:

"To-day is the day that Sir Richard of Lea must come and pay the money he owes to the abbey! If not, I shall be able to sell his lands to get back the money he ought to have paid. Now, will he come, or will he not?"

The day before, he had sent a message to the nearest magistrate, asking him to come to the abbey in the morning so that at noon-day he might have a man who stood for Law and Authority on the spot, in order to be a witness that Sir Richard had not paid; for it was at noon that the agreement finished. The Justice had come over the night before willingly enough, for he knew that the Abbot would feed him well, and give him some choice wine. He was not disappointed! The Abbot had done so; for he specially wished to make a friend of the Justice.

After breakfast they did very little but wander around the beautiful grounds of the abbey: and they were beautiful indeed! The monks of the abbey were the gardeners, and as they were gardeners who worked for no pay, there was no need to spare labour and pains. The result was that the lawns were kept like velvet, and the gardens of the abbey were glorious with flowers.

After a little they noticed that the creeping shadow on the sun-dial showed that nine o'clock had come: but Sir Richard of Lea had not, and there were only three hours to noon!

"It does not look as if your expected guest will be here, my lord Abbot!" remarked the Justice. "Perhaps he started out at early dawn to reach the abbey, and his palfrey may have lamed its foot by stumbling into a hole."

"Then he should have allowed time for accidents!", snapped the Abbot. "He should have started out yesterday!"

The Prior laughed. The Prior was the man who next to the Abbot was the chief man at the abbey; and he seemed amused at some thoughts of his own.

"He may even have done that very thing," he remarked. "I can imagine that in these days, Sir Richard may even have left his home to reach here, and had the money with him ready to bring and to pay, but——" Then he paused.

"Then why is he not here?" said the Abbot testily.

"All the same, he may not have it now!" went on the Prior, and there was a world of meaning in his tone.

"Speak plainly, man!" cried the Abbot roughly. "What meanest thou by thy 'he may even have had the money with him, but he may not have it now.' Thou speakest in riddles. Speak plainly, Prior! Do not beat about the bush!"

"*I* am not beating *about* the bush, my lord Abbot!" laughed the Prior. "But Sir Richard may have been beaten *in* the bush. In other words, there are robbers in the forest, and there is a band well known unto us, called Robin Hood and his Merry Men. I meant they may have met Sir Richard of Lea on his way hither: and if so, his men may still be 'merry,' but I trow that Sir Richard is not. Even an' he brought the £400 with him, it may never reach US!"

"I see," said the Abbot thoughtfully. "However, no matter what may hap we will take no excuses. Such things as being robbed on the way, or having his horse lamed, so that he was hindered, may be reasons, but they are no excuses. Is't not so, Mr. Justice?"

"True, quite true, my lord Abbot! Sir Richard hath signed the bond to pay thee the money by noon to-day. Therefore, if the man with the money is here, well and good! If he is not here, or if he is here without the money —then, whatever the reasons he offers, thou mayest sell his lands, and that at once. Certes, they ought to fetch a deal more money than the £400 thou didst lend upon them. Verily, they are worth three times that!"

"May be," sneered the Abbot. "But if it is known that I am selling the land, no one will dare bid against me. They will fall into my

hands for very little more than the £400 he
owes me. Prior! Go into the cloisters and
send one of the monks to the battlement of
the tower to search the roads to see if
Sir Richard of Lea can be beheld in the
distance!"

The Prior did so, and presently the monk
returned answer:

"The roads are clear, but none is near!"
And the shadow of the sundial crept on till
ten o'clock had come, but Sir Richard of Lea
had not! And it wanted but two hours until
noon!

Stronger and stronger grew the hopes in the
mind of the Abbot. Verily it seemed as if
the lands he coveted would soon belong unto
him. And he waited impatiently, and presently
he remarked: "Holy Writ tells us that Joshua
commanded the sun to stand still; but if I
had my way I would make that same sun to
hurry so that our minds may be set at rest
about this business!"

But he could not hurry the sun, and there
was nothing to do but to wait. And the shadow
on the sundial crept forward slowly until eleven
o'clock had come, but Sir Richard of Lea had
not. And it wanted only one hour until noon.

Then a monk came rushing down from the battlements, and dropping upon one knee, exclaimed: "There is an armed knight who hath appeared in the distance, and he is riding in this direction!" And it wanted but fifteen

minutes more when the knight rode up to the gates of the abbey, and knocked upon it. To him the porter opened, and he rode through on the fine steed which had been provided for him by Robin Hood and his Merry Men. On he came through the grounds which led up to the main buildings of the abbey, and when he caught sight of the Abbot standing there with the Prior and the Justice, he dismounted and knelt before him in reverence.

The Abbot wasted no time in getting down to business, and said roughly:

"There is not much time until noon, Sir Richard of Lea! Hast thou brought me the money that will discharge thy debt?"

"It will not take long to pay it over to thee," answered the knight, "if I am able to pay it. Nor will it take thee long to agree to take a part of it, and to grant me another year to pay the rest. Meanwhile, my lord Abbot, wilt thou not give me thy blessing?" And, as he knelt, the knight was able to hide the smile upon his face: for he was chuckling.

"I am not here to parley with thee," quoth the Abbot. "Neither am I here to take half thy debt. In very truth, all I will have, and not one penny less! Neither will I grant thee any time! At noon to-day either the abbey has thy money, or it has thy lands. We will come into the office of the abbey, and there we will settle the matter." Saying this, he waddled towards the building, and in a few moments the Abbot sat in his big chair and the Justice and the Prior sat on his right hand and his left.

"Now, Sir Knight, we will waste no time. We are not here to listen to excuses, nor to parley. To-day thou must pay thy gold to my hands, or those same hands will seize on thy lands." But he did not want the money, he wanted to lay his hands upon the estates of Sir Richard, so that he could get them cheaply.

Then the knight flung back his head, and tugging at the back of his belt, he untied from thence, where his head had it hidden all the time under his fine coat, a bag which was heavy with coins. The Abbot stared and frowned in perplexity. Was it possible, he wondered, that Sir Richard could pay him the money after all?

Sir Richard did! He undid the bag and poured out the four hundred pieces of gold which Robin Hood had lent him, and then he said bluntly, turning to the Justice:

"Verily, I am glad thou art here, Sir Justice, for thou canst be witness both that there are four hundred pieces of gold to be counted, and that everyone of them is good. There are still ten minutes before noon of this day, so I have kept my word, and I will trouble thee to see that my lord Abbot doth hand over to me the deed I signed, so that I come into my own again!"

The Justice nodded. He counted the money, and behold, it was the right amount!—he tested each piece of gold, and behold, it was good! "I am a witness that Sir Richard hath paid!" he said to the Abbot. "Give him the deed!" And when the knight rode away he had it with him!

So the tables were turned!

HOW THE PRIOR RETURNED
SIR RICHARD'S MONEY

THE Abbot of St. Mary's felt a much injured man on the day that Sir Richard of Lea paid him £400 in gold to redeem his lands from debt. In his heart he wondered how it was that the knight had come through Sherwood Forest without being robbed by Robin Hood and his Merry Men: but that he had done so showed him that it was safe to pass through the forest. So he took the four hundred pieces of gold, and very much more money that had been paid him as rents by the retainers of the abbey, and when he had added them together, he saw they made £800.

It was an enormous sum of money: but the Abbot could do no good with it while it was lying there. If only he could place it in the hands of some of the goldsmiths and merchants in Nottingham, they could use it, and pay him forty or fifty pounds a year for doing so.

He sent for the Prior, and, pointing to the gold, he said:

"This money is lying here idle; so I am going to get thee to take it all to the merchants of Nottingham, and there are several mule packs of goods which have been made by the hands of the monks which you can also take and dispose of in the town!"

"But supposing I fall in with Robin Hood and his Merry Men on the way," the Prior objected. "He would take all the money, and keep it, and the abbey would have neither the money nor the interest."

"It is only lately that he allowed Sir Richard of Lea to pass through with £400," said the Abbot. "But as it is as well to be on the safe side, I will send with thee fifty of the men armed with their bows and arrows, and if any should attack thee they will be able to fight."

The Prior did not like it! He had no stomach for fighting. He was a lover of a quiet life and he looked forward to the journey with positive dismay. However, there was no help for it. Every monk from the Prior downwards was bound by an oath of obedience to the Abbot, and when the Abbot said "You will have to go to

Nottingham!" there was nothing else for it: go he must!

But the Prior was a cunning man, and he thought within himself: "If I take all this gold in money bags and by any chance robbers should surprise us, they would be sure to find the money and seize it. No, that will never do! I will take twenty gold pieces in a bag, as if that were all I have with me; and the rest of the money I will hide up in the packs among the goods on the backs of the mules!"

This he did with much trouble, and none of the men who were with him knew that the money was there. They all thought that the mules were only carrying goods and that the goods were to be sold in Nottingham. Bit by bit the mules were packed and at last they were all ready to start out; and, I can tell you, they looked a right important procession. In front marched twenty of the archers. Mule after mule wended its way slowly along. Then came ten more archers and then some more of the mules. Then, on a comfortable seat, which had been fitted up for him on one of the best mules they possessed, came the Prior, and behind him marched twenty stout men-at-arms. Yes, any man looking on would have said that this was by no means a column which would easily be interfered with; and, to tell the truth, the Prior thought so too.

So they set out, and for the first hour or two everything went well! The mules crept along as mules will; and the men tramped along, with bows ready fitted with arrows, in case of a surprise; and the birds sang around overhead; and wherever the Prior turned his gaze there was nothing but the matchless beauty of the forest glades. Then, as they came out on to an open clearing in the forest and were preparing to cross it in order to enter the forest path on the other side, suddenly, the heart of the Prior sprang into his mouth! A voice cried "Halt!" They looked around and no one could be seen. But they had all heard the voice and they glanced at one another as much as to say, "What shall we do?"

While they were wondering thus, an arrow flew swiftly and buried itself in the bundle of cloth upon which the Prior was sitting, and the Prior himself went as white as a sheet of paper and he made haste to get down off the back of the mule. All the notions he had had of fighting vanished at once. The men who were with him waited in vain for his word of command; and, until he gave it, their leader did not care to take the management of matters upon himself.

So for an instant there was nothing done on either side, and then the invisible voice roared out: "Drop your bows, or if not ye are all dead men: one hundred and fifty of us are around you. We are three to one. Drop your bows."

"Yes, yes, drop your bows, my men!" quavered the Prior in a shaky voice. And very sulkily they slung them across their shoulders once more. Then out of the greenwood Little John and Will Scarlett made their appearance, and one hundred and fifty of Robin Hood's Merry Men stepped forward with their bows ready for instant action.

Little John made his way to the Prior instantly and said:

"Sir Prior! Our leader, Robin Hood, has sent us to invite you and your men to join us in a merry meal. He heard that ye were for Nottingham on business bent and he wondered whether ye would not satisfy your hunger and quench your thirst ere ye go farther to sell your goods."

The Prior pricked up his ears. It seemed to him quite clear that the packs of the mules had led Robin Hood astray as to the chief business which he had in hand. Little John had only referred to the goods that he was taking to Nottingham.

So far so good! So long as the money was safe nothing else mattered very much, and he answered Little John that if he would lead the way to his master he would follow with his men.

An hour later they were all gathered around the festive board. Robin Hood had made the Prior right welcome; but when the meal had gone apace and they had all well eaten and drunk, Robin exclaimed to the Prior:

"It is generally the custom of my guests to contribute something towards the cost of such meals as they have with us. If it is a poor man he gets it for nothing. But if he is a man of substance then he payeth heavily both for the meal he has had and for those who before him have had theirs free. So, Sir Prior, tell me, I prithee, what thou art inclined to pay for thyself and these men of thine."

The Prior spoke smoothly as he said:

"Thou seest that we are but on our outward
journey. We have not as yet sold our goods.
Had we been returning it would have been a
different matter. Ye know that monks like

myself are but poor folk! And, verily, I have
but a sum of about twenty gold pieces with me
for the expenses of my men and myself in
Nottingham. It cannot be in thine heart to
take that from us and to leave us stranded.

So, verily, I and my men must cast ourselves upon thy favour."

"With all my heart," quoth Robin. "If thou wilt certify me that is all the money that thou hast, then thy meal and the meal of thy men shall be given ye all. But is it so?" And he looked at the Prior keenly.

However, the Prior stuck to his story and Robin appeared to accept it. But suddenly he turned to the Prior, saying:

"Sir Prior, whilst thou hast been feeding, some of my men have searched thy packs upon the back of thy mules, and it was [as though we had walked into a treasury of gold. Sir Prior, thou hast tried to deceive me! Had'st thou told the truth I would have scorned to lay hands upon the money of trustful men. As it is thou must pay for thy men—there are fifty of them with big appetites—and for thyself, with the biggest appetite of them all. I shall but charge ye five pound apiece for the meal, and we shall be glad to see ye again some other day. Five pounds apiece for fifty makes £250, and there will be a trifle of a fine of £150 on thyself, because thou didst try to deceive me. That is £400, and as thou didst have £800 I will return thee the half and keep the other half."

It was but useless to protest, and the poor Prior went off with only half the money, a sadder and wiser man.

But some months later when Sir Richard of Lea came to return the money he had borrowed of Robin Hood to pay the Abbot with, Robin told him that the debt was already paid, for the Prior had returned the money on his way to Nottingham. "Keep thy money in thy pocket!" quoth Robin, "and if thou hast some boys, save it against the time when thou hast to start them out into the world."

HOW ALLIN-A-DALE JOINED ROBIN'S BAND

ONE day Robin Hood was walking out with a couple of his men, Little John and Much, the miller's son. They journeyed until they reached the bridle-path that wended through the Forest. There they cast themselves down under the greenwood tree to watch from their hiding-place any who might come or go.

They often did this, though sometimes none passed either way, or those that did were not worthy of notice. But this particular morning Robin caught sight of a strapping young man, who was dressed in scarlet that closely fitted his sturdy form; and as he went along he sang at the top of his voice a ballad of the day.

Robin looked at him, and sighed with envy; and turning, he said to Little John:

"I would give a great deal to be as happy as he. It's many a day since I walked like that, and whistled and sang for the mere joy of being alive!"

He went back to the camp with the twain, but he could not forget the blithe young man he had seen. It reminded him so much of the day when he, too, was free from care, and sang because he need not sigh.

A week later he again went in the same direction with his two companions: and, much to his surprise, Robin Hood espied the same youth. Robin remembered him at once. But he was much changed. To-day he had on some shabby old clothes as though he were careless how he appeared. He no longer walked with a spring and a whistle, and no song came from his lips. He moved as though it were a trouble to live.

"Only a week!" quoth Robin. "Only a week to make a change like this. There is trouble afoot in that young man's life. This must be seen into!" And, turning to Little John, and Much the miller's son, he said: "Fetch him hither to me!"

They obeyed quickly, but as soon as the young man heard their steps upon the bracken he unslung his bow and stood on guard.

"What do you want with me?" he cried

suspiciously. But they quickly calmed his fears, and told him that Robin wished to see him.

A moment or two later he stood facing Robin, who looked at him mischievously, and said: "But a week sin' I saw thee stepping along blithely, clothed in brave attire, and thou didst sing a roundelay as thou didst walk, and thou didst walk as if thou wert treading on air. To-day thou art but going along as though all the trouble of the world were on thy shoulders. Now, tell me, why is this?"

The young man looked at Robin, and made answer:

"How else should it be? When I sang, a week sin', I sang because in a few days the girl I loved was to have married me. Yes, even yesterday. But to-morrow she is to be taken from me, and is to be given by her father to a grave and sober knight old enough to be her father; and, verily, I feel as if my heart were broken."

"O-ho!" said Robin. "No wonder thou art sad! What is thy name, O bridegroom-that-was-to-be?"

"Men call me Allin-a-Dale!" he replied.

"Well, Allin-a-Dale," Robin went on, "where is this marriage of thy maid with this worshipful old knight to take place?"

"It is but five miles as the road winds!" answered the youth. "But what is there that can be done?" sadly.

"What wilt thou give me and my Merry Men," said Robin Hood, "if I snatch thy maiden to-morrow from this cruel fate, and give her unto thee?"

"There is nothing I can give thee," said the youth. "I am but starting out in life, and have saved nothing. The maid and I were going to save together; and everything looked rosy to lovers like ourselves. Yet, if thou wilt do this thing I will take oath to become one of ye, and serve ye with might and main."

"So be it!" cried Robin. "Now, Allin-a-Dale, do thou return to thine own home and say nought to any man. But when to-morrow morn shall have come, hie thee to the church, dressed in all thy brave attire, and there thou shalt meet my Merry Men and myself; and if there be a disappointed man go away from that church, verily it will not be thyself. Canst thou get a note to the maiden to tell her that it will be all right; for it may be that she is troubling her heart even as thou art."

And Allin-a-Dale said that he could and would.

"Now, advise me just where the church may be found!" cried Robin; and Allin-a-Dale did so, and Robin promised that he would be there.

The morning dawned. The knight who was to be married by the girl of Allin-a-Dale, in obedience to her father, rose early and remembered with glee of heart that to-day was his wedding-day; and he put on his most glittering array as became a wealthy knight.

But Robin Hood had also remembered his promise, and early did he sally forth from the camp, carrying with him a harp, at which his men laughed, for they knew he could not play a note upon its strings. But having given them their orders as to what they should do, away he rambled, taking a short path through the Forest which he knew, until he came to the little church where Allin had told him the wedding was to be.

He strode into the church as though he were one of the travelling minstrels who wandered through the land. No one took any notice of

D

his presence, it was such a usual sight, and a welcome one, to behold one of these minstrels. But, presently, the Bishop who was waiting to join the couple in marriage, called to him to give them some music.

"I cannot play," quoth Robin, "until the sight of the bride and the bridegroom shall make my heart gay. Then I will play indeed." And the folk who were in the church smiled at one another, and waited for the arrival of the maid and the old knight.

It wanted some time before they put in an appearance. First came the rich old knight, whose form was the form of one who had seen many years, and, at length, there came the bride, whom they had clothed in bright attire, but whose face was white with excitement.

Then, as they marched up to the altar, the strange minstrel fell in behind them; and as the Bishop made ready with his book, the minstrel slipped to the front and faced the folk in the church.

"I do protest," said Robin, in a loud voice, "that this is no fit match. May and December can never agree. Far better is it that since we are come into the church for a wedding, the bride shall be allowed to choose her own groom."

Then, dropping the harp upon which he knew not how to play, Robin put his horn to his

lips, on which he could play full well; and when he had blown his well-known call four-and-twenty bowmen, led by Little John, came leaping to his summons. Through the church-yard, and up the church, marching two by two they came; and then Robin turned to Allin-a-Dale, saying:

"Here is thy true love, and you shall be married in this same place, and this same hour, before we leave the building."

Pale of face with the anger he felt, the Bishop cried aloud: "This shall never be! There have been no banns published between them: they must be asked three times in church before they can be married; for that is the law of the land and of the Church!"

Robin Hood wasted no time, but ordered Little John to pull off the Bishop's robe and mitre, and put them on to Friar Tuck, who was a priest. "Thou shalt be Bishop," quoth Robin, "and thou shalt wed the twain."

Friar Tuck went up into the choir, and the people began to laugh, as instead of three times, he called the couple's names seven times, lest three should not be enough. Then he cried aloud: "Who gives this maid unto this man?" And in the silence which followed, Robin Hood cried:

"I do! I, Robin Hood. Gentleman-at-arms of Sherwood Forest, near by. I do!"

But here the old knight, who had been intent upon wedding her, cried: "I forbid this lawless marriage!" But, at a gesture from Robin his Merry Men hustled around him, and gently pushed him down the aisle and out of the door of the church.

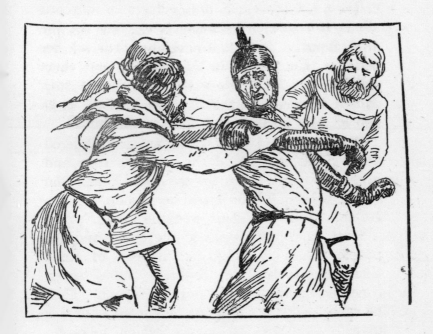

When he had gone the mock Bishop went on with the service, and at the end of it he pronounced Allin-a-Dale and his true love, man and wife, to live together for better for worse, for richer for poorer.

Then Robin Hood cried:

"Let it be known that anyone, be he high or low, who tries to take her from Allin-a-Dale will pay for her very dearly!"

Then the bride and the bridegroom marched down the aisle arm-in-arm, and they set the bride upon a palfrey, and Allin-a-Dale led her back to the camp in the Forest; and there Allin-a-Dale kept his word, and served with Robin Hood and his Merry Men as long as he would, and his own true love served him.

LITTLE JOHN'S JOKE

You will scarcely believe that during all this time that Robin Hood had been with his Merry Men since he went into the Forest there was one bitter enemy still determined to capture him if he could: I mean the Sheriff of Nottingham.

He still kept him proclaimed as an outlaw, and never a complaint reached him about any further mischief which Robin Hood had worked but he had another hue-and-cry made. He hated the very mention of Robin's name: for it was the name of a man who had escaped him and his officers so far: and he felt himself the laughing-stock of the whole county. He would have paid anything to lay Robin by the heels and to break up his band. It was his dearest desire, except one: and that was that amongst his own men he might have some of the finest archers in the whole of England. Yes, hatred of Robin Hood and love of archery were the two ruling crazes of his life.

Robin Hood and his men knew it and they returned the hatred: and while the Sheriff was racking his brains to take Robin, Robin and his Merry Men were racking theirs to get even with him.

Little John especially kept a grudge against the man who persecuted his master, and at last he formed a pretty little plot in his mind how to play a joke upon the Sheriff. The plan was this.

One of the richest knights who lived near the Forest was Sir Richard of Lea. Some time back Sir Richard had got into trouble with the Abbot of St. Mary's over some money he owed the Abbot. But Robin Hood had lent it to him, so that he paid the Abbot in time, and saved his lands, which would have been forfeit. He never forgot the kindness of Robin and his Merry Men, and after he had paid Robin back the money he still remained their fast friend.

So to him Little John hied himself one day and said:

"In good sooth, Sir Richard, I'm getting tired of being always in the Forest and I've a rare wish to take service with thee."

Sir Richard was puzzled, but Little John went on:

"Methinks this dress of Lincoln green is no longer suitable, and I have a great desire to see how I look in the scarlet and white which thine own men wear."

Then a light broke in upon Sir Richard. He saw that in reality Little John wanted to disguise himself. Why he did not know, neither did Little John tell him.

For some time Little John stayed with him as one of his yeoman archers, and where they went he went, which was what Little John heartily wished. And it fell out even as he expected.

In the course of a month or two some great sports were to be held in Nottingham, and the yeoman archers of Sir Richard of Lea would be sure to go to try for the prizes. They went, and, laughing heartily—for Sir Richard began to see what Little John was after—he allowed that good man to go with them:—as one of the company clad in the livery of scarlet and white.

Little dreamed the townsmen of Nottingham, as they saw Little John's wonderful feats at the shooting match, that they had amongst them one of the outlaws of Sherwood Forest. But the Sheriff was amazed at his skill and could scarcely contain himself till the match was over, so that he could come down from his seat and try to buy this wondrous archer to enter his own service.

At first Little John made pretence to be unwilling; but the Sheriff offered him high wages, and then still higher, until at last he yielded, provided his present master, Sir Richard, would consent.

"Oh, I will see to him!" quoth the Sheriff. "Tell me thy name and I will make request for thee."

"The men do call me Reynold Greenleaf," said Little John. And it was true, for under that name he had entered Sir Richard's service.

"Then, Reynold Greenleaf, thou shalt be one of my archers and servants and I will pay thee double thou gettest now, and feed thee, and clothe thee, and find thee lodgings with the rest."

And he made haste to make requests of Sir Richard of Lea to allow this wonderful archer to depart and to come to him.

Then Sir Richard understood how Little John had planned this all along, and let him go.

With his sides shaking with laughter he went in and told his good lady:

"Verily the Sheriff will rue the day when

he took my best archer away." And he went
on to tell her the joke, at which she laughed
heartily also—for she detested the Sheriff more
than any other in the district, save one, and

that one was the Sheriff's lady -a proud and
pompous dame.

So Little John entered the Sheriff's service
and his house; and for a little all went well.
But Little John was only biding his time.

He found the Sheriff was a mean man, who kept him waiting for his money and gave his men poor kind of fare and little enough of that, and the new servant just waited for his chance.

It fell upon a day that the Sheriff of Nottingham went out to a distant town upon business bent, and he took with him many of his men, but Little John was left behind. Now, in the bustle of getting off, those who were going made but a hasty repast, and they who stayed, like "Reynold Greenleaf," were left to the mercy of the steward to provide them their breakfast.

Now the steward was a lazy man, and as mean as he was lazy; nor was he averse from saving meals by leaving men hungry and charging in his accounts as though he had served them.

But he did not know Reynold Greenleaf, although he and the rest did not favour the new-comer, for the simple reason that their master see~ ed to.

In the mia-morning Reynold Greenleaf put his head into the pantr and asked for something to eat and drink.

"I have not yet broken my fast and there is a cry within me that will not be denied. Food must I have, and that right soon, Sir Steward!"

"Then get it," quoth the steward. "But 'twill not be from me. I cannot leave my better work to wait upon such as thyself. Nor will I! Were our master here he would dine at eventide.

Wait till then! And, meanwhile, take thyself out!"

"Not till I have cracked thy head!" cried Reynold Greenleaf furiously. And he made for the steward roughly, but the steward fled. Yet before he could get through the door

Reynold Greenleaf fetched him such a buffet on the head that he fell into a corner and lay there. Whereupon Reynold Greenleaf walked into the place and helped himself to a fine meal.

But in the very midst of his meal in came the cook, a brave and burly man, who had heard the sound of the struggle and the heavy fall of the steward and came to see what these things meant.

In a moment he saw the truth, and rushing at the new servant he dealt him two or three hard blows.

Then Reynold Greenleaf, or Little John, swung his staff, and the cook seized another, and they fell to thwacking each other for nigh half an hour, and to his surprise Little John found he had met his match.

Now, as they paused to rest, Little John exclaimed: "Thou art a right good hand with thy staff. If thou could'st shoot just as well with a bow, I would ask thee to go back with me to the Forest and become one of Robin Hood's Merry Men."

"And who art thou to make me such an offer?" said the cook curiously.

"Men call me Little John!" said he. And at once the cook began to roar with laughter at the trick by which this hated man had got into his master's service.

"Verily, I will go with thee!" he cried. "But it must be right soon, before the steward collects his scattered wits."

And they shook hands on it.

"But," quoth Little John, "let us not go empty-handed. That were a poor thing to do. The Sheriff owes me some wages."

"And he owes me some more!" cried the cook.

"Then let us pay ourselves and" (chuckling) "charge the Sheriff high interest." So they tore through to the Sheriff's private room and broke open desks and table-drawers and gathered a bag of silver and three hundred pounds in gold, and cramming them into two sacks they carried them off and made their way into the Forest.

Back through the old familiar paths Little John struggled under his heavy load, and the burly cook toiled on behind him; until at length they came in sight of the clearing, and there, round the campfire, as of old, sat Robin Hood and his Merry Men.

They sprang to their feet as the two men staggered towards them, both of them dressed in the Sheriff's colours.

"Now, who and what have we here?" cried Robin.

Then said Little John:

"O master, but I am glad to be back!"

And the men broke into a roar of cheers, and when they heard the story they cheered still more.

ROBIN HOOD AND THE SHERIFF
OF NOTTINGHAM

LITTLE JOHN was dancing about full of merriment. It was on the morning of the day after his return to the Forest. He had returned from playing a prank upon the Sheriff, having got into his house as his archer; he had just left it with the Sheriff's cook and his silver dishes. He was dancing for he had suddenly thought of a daring plan by which he could bring the hated Sheriff into the greenwood as a guest of Robin Hood.

So he stepped up to his master:

"Wilt thou see to it, O master, that the silver dishes which I brought from the Sheriff's house yester-eve, are made ready to serve a meal to the Sheriff himself some time to-day? And see to it that that great gawky cook of his waits upon him when he comes!"

Robin Hood looked at him with puzzled face.

"Verily, I do not understand thee, Little John!" he cried.

"No, master! But when a few hours have gone by take it, from me that thou wilt."

So away ran Little John, and dressed himself once more in the attire of the Sheriff's men, and then turned his feet as rapidly as he could to meet the Sheriff himself, as he would return towards his own home in Nottingham that very morning.

One mile he went, and then two. But still there was no Sheriff! The two miles had become three, and then it happened to him just as he had expected and as he desired. He came upon the Sheriff himself, who was returning on his way homewards, and using the chance that his journey gave him to hunt in the Forest as he went through.

Now the Sheriff of Nottingham was a great huntsman, and Little John knew this. So with perfect confidence he made straight for the Sheriff, who was astounded and not altogether pleased to see him; for he imagined that he was back in Nottingham guarding his home.

"Why art thou here?" demanded the Sheriff roughly.

"May it please you, sir," said Little John, dropping upon his knees, and pulling off his cap, "I heard that you would return this morn, and I guessed right well that thou wouldst be carrying on fine sport on thy way back, and my heart yearned to join in it. It is a long time since my bow went to work under the open sky, and in the glorious greenwood. Forgive me, sir, if I have erred, but when I tell thee what I have seen on my way, I think thou wilt be ready to pardon me."

"Well, varlet, what was it?"

And Little John answered as if he were very excited:

"As I came hither I caught sight of one of the largest harts I have ever seen. He was a giant compared with the usual size of these beasts, and there were with him a herd of many deer, who were following him as their lord and master. I did not dare to shoot, for he looked so wild, and was so immense, that I feared that even if I struck him, the whole herd would turn upon me. It was but a mile or so away that I saw them, and if thou wilt follow me, I can promise thee and thy men some fine sport."

This was enough for the Sheriff, and he remarked instantly:

"I would feign see this enormous beast! So Reynold Greenleaf"—calling Little John by the name by which he knew him—"turn in thy tracks and show me the way."

The Sheriff rode, and Reynold Greenleaf ran beside him, swift of foot. It was not long before they had covered more than a mile, but there was no sign of the beast; and then Reynold Greenleaf protested that the hart and his herd must have gone further off, and, all unsuspecting, the Sheriff went with him in order to track the beast. On and on they went with all a huntsman's ardour for sport, till presently, as they dashed through the greenwood, they came out into an open glade, and there, under an enormous tree, sat Robin Hood and one hundred and fifty of his Merry Men.

The Sheriff turned upon Reynold Greenleaf in bitterness, for he saw that he had been trapped; but it was too late for him to do anything, for the men came forward at once and insisted that the Sheriff should dismount and have a meal with them.

Robin Hood welcomed him with courtesy,

but there was a gleam in his eyes which made
the Sheriff feel uncomfortable inside. But as
there was no help for it he sat him down to eat
and to drink, wondering in his heart what Robin
Hood would do with the man who had proclaimed all through the county a reward for
him dead or alive.

It was not long before the meal was served,
and when the Sheriff saw that he was eating
off a service of fine silver which he at
once knew was his own, he groaned in spirit.
Nor was this the worst that befell him, for
looking up he caught sight of his own cook
bringing in the dishes, and he saw at once
that he had been robbed and betrayed. The
others ate and enjoyed their meal, but the
Sheriff had a poor appetite that day.

Then he looked at his enemy straight in the
face, for the Sheriff was no coward, and said:
"You have trapped me in a base manner
and I see that thy men have also robbed me
of my silver, so now tell me what thou art
going to do with me?"

"Make you wear the green dress of my
Merry Men," he replied. And turning to his
men he bade them strip the Sheriff of his costly
attire and dress him in one of their own mantles.

And then he insisted that the Sheriff should
stay there with them and see for himself how
the man and the men he hated spent their
nights. It was in vain that the Sheriff made

protest, for as the evening shadows drew on
apace, they made him lie down on the hard
ground in their midst, and in good sooth the
Sheriff had never had a harder bed. He turned
and he twisted but he could not sleep, and

after hours of this wretched experience he was ready to make promises of anything if only Robin Hood and his men would let him go away home.

"What do you think of our hardy way of spending the night?" asked Robin Hood at the morning meal. And the Sheriff answered: "Not for anything would I have another such night as this."

"Ah, but thou wilt," cried Robin, winking at his Merry Men. "Thou shalt verily stay with us for twelve months."

"Nay," cried the Sheriff. "I must ask thy mercy."

"Wouldst thou have shown us any?" quoth Robin.

"None at all!" answered the Sheriff.

Then Robin Hood, who, if the Sheriff had proved to be a coward, would have done his worst with him, went over to his Merry Men and talked it over with them. "What shall be done with this enemy of ours whom Little John has delivered into our hands. We do not want his money and we do not want his life as he did ours: what shall be done with him?"

And some said one thing and some another.

Some were for flogging him as he would have flogged them. Little John spoke up then and said:

"If he had wandered our way and been caught

that would be a different thing. But I misled him into coming here and I like not the thought of flogging a man whom I have trapped. We have his silver, and his cook has joined our band, and he hath learned what the Merry Men are like. I counsel, O master, that thou shouldst exact a promise from him to leave us unmolested for the future, and then when he has thus sworn, to let him go free."

As they all agreed to this Robin went back to the Sheriff and told him:

"Thou camest here as our enemy: but we are men who do not wish to take thy life. We would rather turn thee into a friend. Thou art in our power, and, as thou seest, we might verily take thy life. But we spare thee. And because we do think it but fair that before we send thee hence, without asking thee for ransom or any such thing that thou shouldst swear friendship to us for ever. We do but wish that thou shouldst leave us alone. Wilt give me thy promise?"

A light gleamed in the Sheriff's eyes.

"Verily it is more than I should have done for thee!" he cried. "But I see now that thou art a man, and I will be thy friend as thou sayest. I will make no more proclamations about thee—thou art no longer to me 'Robin Hood, the outlaw'—thou art and ever will be the MAN-WHO-SPARED-MY-LIFE."

So Robin Hood and his Merry Men sent the

Sheriff away, and lo, he kept his word right loyally; but often as he sat at table and missed the fine silver that once he had had, he wished he only had Reynold Greenleaf in his hand. Which was only natural.

THE SHERIFF SETS A TRAP

IF anyone had told Robin Hood that if he captured the Sheriff of Nottingham he would let him go, he would never have believed it. However, he did! He let him go! And the Sheriff went back a friendly man—a changed man.

However, the good wife could not at all understand the way her lord and master seemed to take the matter. Never a day passed but she fumed and fretted as she dined off plain earthenware dishes, or dishes of pewter, instead of the fine silver she had had once.

"How canst thou put up with it?" quoth she. "Here is this band of outlaws in the King's forest still, and there they have been for a long time, and yet nothing is done against them!"

"And nothing shall be done!" he said roughly. "Have I not told thee, woman, that when I was in the power of his hand, Robin Hood let

me go, and that without ransom? Why, in
these days of violence, such a thing hath been
unknown! Knight holds to ransom other
knights; and noble does the same with noble;
even King Richard was held in prison till the
kingdom paid his captor a goodly sum. Yet
this man set me free and asked nothing! I
will take no step against him, I say."

"But he did make thee pay ransom," she
persisted. "Did he not have some hundreds of
pounds worth of thy silver plate? What was
that but ransom?"

"That is one way of looking at the matter,
dame!" he answered. "And what thou sayest
is right enough, but I have given my word, and
I cannot go back on it."

"But if I could show thee a way to get quit
of thy promise," she insisted, "without losing
thine honour, wouldst thou take it?"

"Ay, that would I!" he cried right heartily.
"If ever some fair chance delivered Robin Hood
into mine hand, so that I could set him free in
the same way, we should be quits, and I could
try to take him again after that!"

Whereupon his wife set her wits to work;
and, first of all, she did get friends of hers to
send letters unto the King complaining that

Robin and his Merry Men went unmolested,
and that the Sheriff did not seem able to
lay them by the heels. And when the King
did receive these letters, he was exceeding
angry, and sent messengers to the Sheriff,
saying:

"Thou must rid me and my forest of these
outlaws, or thou mayest be no longer Sheriff!"

Now when the Sheriff did receive these
messages, he was sore troubled in mind, and
showed them unto his wife.

"What did I tell thee?" she cried. "And now,
while thou dost refuse to do anything, thou
wilt give offence to the King. He needs must
remove thee from thy office; for how doth
he know thou art not hand in glove with them
thyself? Other men in high place at this time
have made common cause with robbers, and
doubtless the King says to himself: 'How do I
know the Sheriff of Nottingham is not as one
like to them?'"

The Sheriff looked at her in amaze. He had
never thought of this! He seemed very worried
by it, too; and, at last, he cried: "Then,
woman, tell me what I must do?"

She had her plans all ready in her mind,
and now she told him what they were. And the

Sheriff laughed as if he were very pleased, saying:

"I will do this thing. I will, perhaps, capture Robin Hood. And if he escapes, as I want to let him do, so as to keep my word—after that we shall be quits, and then, ah then I will hunt him to death."

The plans of the Sheriff's wife soon bore fruit. News flew through the County of Nottingham—why, they even spread to Robin Hood and his Merry Men—that there was to be a great shooting match held in the town of Nottingham itself. The shooting was to be with bows and arrows, and the prize was one so valuable that even the best archers would try for it. It was to be a solid silver arrow with a head of gold.

When Robin Hood and his Merry Men heard that, they made up their minds to go to the place and strive in the match for the victory; and, as they were all archers of skill, and decided that only the best amongst themselves should try their hands, it looked very hopeful.

Now the Sheriff had planned this match because he knew it would provoke Robin and his Merry Men to try and win the prize. That was just a mere bit of bait to tempt the fish to bite. He wanted Robin and Little John and some of the best archers to come to the match. It was his wife's plan, and it was just the plan that worked; but Robin was quite as cute as the Sheriff, and decided that he and one hundred of his Merry Men would go forth disguised; so that if they were looking for men dressed in Lincoln Green, find them they would not. Therefore twenty-five men dressed in white, twenty-five in red, twenty-five in yellow, and twenty-five in blue. Each carried a quiver full of arrows, the best arrows in their armoury; just the best seasoned wood, just the right weight of feather-tip, and all the strings of their bows were tested for their strength and spring. Away they went, and as they drew near to Nottingham, they found that all the townsfolk were pouring out towards the meadow in which the match was to be held. At one end they had put up a wand made of willow, and it was this which was to be the target. Near the target special stands full of seats had been provided for all the gentry, and nobles, and knights of the county, and their wives and daughters. But the crowd stood all around the field behind the ropes.

The Merry Men from the greenwood mixed

with the rest who were going to shoot, and as there were eight hundred archers taking part, they were easily overlooked. But while the best of Robin's men took part in the contest, the others kept their bows and arrows ready, in case of any attempt to capture their leader and his men.

It took a long time for the failures to drop out, till the eight hundred had become half, and the four hundred had become two hundred, and the two hundred one hundred, and the one hundred had become fifty, and the fifty had become five. All of these five, unknown to the townsfolk, belonged to Robin Hood's band.

Meanwhile the Sheriff was disappointed; for he had made certain that Robin Hood would turn up.

The five men tried their skill, and one of them fell out, and then there were four. The four became three, the three two, and at last Robin himself was left, and he had won the prize.

He stepped up to receive it, but in the crowd who sat with the Sheriff there was an old knight who had been Robin Hood's guest by force, and he recognised him, and told the Sheriff, who immediately gave the alarm aloud,

but he whispered to Robin Hood to fly. And
thus he kept his word to Robin, and cried
"quits."

But the alarm had sounded, and at once

there was a great struggle. Robin and his
men shot their arrows fast and thick, and
broke through the line of the Sheriff's men.
However, they did not all escape, and Little
John was shot right through the knee, so that
he could not move.

E

He would have been taken for certain, but, with his immense strength, Robin picked him up and carried him over his shoulder, and bore him away. And whenever he was tired of his burden he laid him upon the ground, while he and his Merry Men went on shooting at their pursuers; and many of those who were following them bit the dust.

It was a long way back to their forest: and it is doubtful if they would ever have reached it, but Robin Hood remembered that the castle of Sir Richard of Lea was nearer, and he knew that out of gratitude for what he had done for him once, that good knight would take them in.

While this very thought was in his mind, and he was making for the castle, Sir Richard came spurring by, and shouted to Robin to bring all his men within the walls.

The greater part of them got there safely, and Sir Richard and his good lady made them all welcome, and made them stay.

So they escaped out of the hand of the Sheriff, in the safety and protection of the castle walls.

The Sheriff was not sorry that so it had happened. Now he was quits with Robin Hood,

and therefore free from his word. He called
a meeting at once of the knights and nobles
of the district, and it was decided to make an

outlaw of Sir Richard of Lea, because he had
befriended the outlaws of the forest.

It was also agreed that the Sheriff of Nottingham should go up by road to London immediately, and tell the King what had happened.

When the King heard of it, he made up his
mind to go to Nottingham himself, and deal

with these men and the bold knight who had set the King's law at defiance.

But London was more than a hundred miles off, and it took five days to go, and the same time to return, and several days for the King to get ready, and meanwhile, Little John rested his knee till it got better, and presently he and the rest of the Merry Men, and Sir Richard of Lea, who had gone with the band, were once more under the greenwood tree.

ROBIN HOOD IS HUNTED

THE news reached the King while he was preparing to come and take Robin Hood, that he and his men and Sir Richard of Lea were once more in the heart of the Sherwood Forest country around Nottingham and that, once he was there, right in the midst of their forest home, it would be little use attempting to trace and find them.

Then the King bit his lip in his annoyance, and walked up and down his chamber like a wild animal which was angry; until at last his feelings burst out and he shouted:

"Is there then no one of all my knights and nobles who can rid me of this pestilent fellow? What! is he and his Merry Men to be merry at my expense? His fires lit with wood from my trees and his food furnished forth from my deer? And, in addition, robbing travellers who pass through? What! shall such a man escape, while I am supposed to rule this land. Never, never! NEVER!"

He meant it too, and the next day there was a saddling of many horses, and the arming of many knights, and the tramp, tramp, tramp of many men as they all marched off from the great city to the country to settle matters with Robin Hood. And in the midst of them rode the King himself. Yes, he meant that there should be no bungling this time.

On they rode: on and on until they came by the banks of the silvery River Trent, when they had marched over one hundred and twenty miles. There they made for themselves a camp, and there they were joined by the knights and nobles of the district and their archers and followers, until there was a mighty crowd.

Then the King made proclamation:

"Now, be it known unto you that whosoever will take Robin Hood alive or dead, shall receive his freedom and a grant of land if he be a serf; and if he be a knight, he shall have added to all the lands he then owneth the lands of that rascally knight, Sir Richard of

Lea, which are hereby declared to be forfeit. And until Robin Hood and Sir Richard of Lea are taken or slain, then they are declared to be enemies and outlaws. No man is to give them food, nor drink, nor shelter; or if they shall they will be heavily fined and be cast into prison, there to abide at the pleasure of the King."

There were many copies made of this proclamation and put up on the doors of churches and read to the people by those few who could read; and they were also sent to the knights of the district to be read to their own folk. And, meanwhile, the King put a wall of his followers around the road of the Forest, so that Robin Hood could not break out; and day by day he drew that circle of armed men tighter and tighter.

Many of these proclamations bold Robin Hood read, and he laughed over them with his Merry Men. And now began a game—a great game of hide-and-seek. Sometimes the King and his men were "warm," and almost found the men for whom they were seeking; but Robin and his men were so used to the ways of the Forest that they could have travelled them even in the dark, or even if they had been blindfolded. So they slipped aside out of the snare.

One month had gone, two, four, and at last six whole months; and still the confident King was beaten. The game was still going on and the man had not been found. Where could he be? Where were his men? It was a puzzle!

But one day there came to the King a forester who, dropping upon his knee, suggested to the King that, if the King wished to see Robin Hood himself, he had thought of a plan whereby it could be done. And when the King had listened he thought it a capital plan, and he and five knights made haste to the abbey and borrowed the long gowns of the monks, and as for the King he also borrowed the hat of the Abbot, and when they had dressed themselves in this fashion, they set off into the forest. For the plan was this. It was well known that Robin loved to rob the monks, and the sight of them travelling with well-filled pouches would prove a tempting bait. If it did, the King was a mighty man and felt that he could give an account of himself in a struggle with Robin Hood that would be quite satisfactory.

So away they rode, and it turned out even as they had thought. Robin and his men met them and in their usual way invited them to take a meal with them. Which thing the King and his knights consented to do. There was no help for it! For they saw themselves surrounded by the archers in goodly array and they were in the power of their hand.

The meal was spread, and presently, as the King saw the plenty and profusion of it, he said:

"But it is not long since that I read a proclamation of the King's majesty that no one should provide ye with bread to eat or liquor to drink. How, then, cometh this feast?"

"Sir Abbot," Robin replied, "there are hearts which have a soft place in them for myself and my Merry Men and they would not see me without bread nor wine. We are all from this district and the folk are our folk and we are theirs."

After the meal was over Robin politely asked them to pay what they could towards the cost thereof; and the pretended Abbot handed to him a purse of gold pieces; out of which Robin

took half and generously handed back half
to his guest again.

"It is very good of you," quoth the Abbot.
"And now, before you let me go, I would be

glad if you would let me see your men at your
revels, of which I have heard."

Robin Hood looked pleased at the interest
and courtesy of his guest. He immediately
blew a horn and the whole of his band came

around and dropped upon one knee as though he, Robin, was some great noble, or even a monarch. At which the King himself was surprised. Then, at a word from Robin, they set up a target which was arranged so that whoever would shoot at it must stand much farther off than the King had ever seen any marksman stand. Moreover, between the target in which was the bull's-eye and those who would shoot there was placed a small hoop, and behind that a still smaller; so that he who would strike the target would have to send his arrow through the hoops and then unerringly reach the bulls'-eye of the target behind. It was a test of skill sufficient to daunt the cleverest archers in the land, and the King in his heart did not believe that it could be done, and so he said.

But Robin only laughed, and turning to his men declared that whoever missed that target must get a buffet on the head from the man who won. This was a game, just in the rough fashion to please the King; and he watched it with great amusement. Robin and one other were the victors, and at last Robin missed; and instead of allowing his man to give him the buffet on the head, he strode up to the Abbot and demanded jokingly that he should give it him. Little he dreamed that he was inviting one of the strongest arms in the world to smite him. But when he had received the

blow he knew it was no ordinary strength which had struck it. He looked at his guest with great respect, and said, "It is a pity you cannot shoot, Sir Abbot, as well as you can smite."

But the pretended Abbot took up a bow and fitted an arrow to it to see what he could do, and as he did so the cowl he had worn over his head fell back; and Sir Richard of Lea, who had seen the King many times, knew him instantly and doffed his hat and fell upon his knee.

Robin Hood was astonished. He hesitated a minute, then, with a sign to his men, he fell upon his knee too and doffed his cap, and so did all the rest.

Silence reigned in that place for a minute or so. Nothing was heard but the twittering of the birds and the swaying of the trees: then Robin broke it:

"My lord the King, thou hast found me at last, and I and my men are at thy mercy: and so art thou at ours! But for the sake of thy kingship and because every son of England loves thy strong arm and stout heart, thou shalt go unmolested. Only we would, before thou dost depart, grant us thy forgiveness and free us from our outlawry. Then thou wouldst verily have no better servants than ourselves."

The King laughed and holding out his hand to Robin forgave him upon condition that he would come to his Court with as many of his men as would follow him. And Robin promised if the King would let him return should he and his men not like the life. And in hearty fashion the King gave his word.

THE KING AND ROBIN HOOD

THE King had hunted Robin Hood and his Merry Men with the forces he had mustered for the purpose, but when he had found that the man and the men he had hunted were really fine fellows, he felt anxious to get their help. Why, it would be like getting another regiment of the finest archers and fighters!

So, when he had pardoned Robin Hood and his Merry Men, and Sir Richard of Lea, he made them promise to come and serve him at his Court.

Now when the promise had been given by Robin that he would come with such of his men as liked to follow, so long as they were allowed to return if the life of the Court did not agree with them, you would have thought the business was all over, and that the King would have gone back again to London.

Well, you would have been wrong.

The King looked around with a merry twinkle

in his eye, and noticed the way in which all of Robin Hood's men were dressed in Lincoln green.

"This dress of yours suits these men right well!" he cried heartily. "Verily, I think I will have some of my archers set forth in the same array."

But as he spoke, those eyes of his twinkled still more, for a sudden thought popped up in his mind like a mischievous imp. And he said to Robin:

"Have you much of this cloth of Lincoln green?" And Robin told him they always kept a good stock of it on hand to use when their garments got old, and also to clothe any new comers.

"Well," quoth the King, "we will be the newcomers! We will buy as much as will make suits for these five knights I have brought with me and for myself." And Robin consented.

There they waited until the best men with the needle had run these suits together; and when the King and the five knights had flung off the monks' robes they had worn when they came into the Forest, they dressed themselves in the new garments.

"Now, my lord the King!" cried Robin. "Tell me, I pray thee, the why and wherefore thou hast done this thing?"

The King laughed merrily.

"I did it because it occurred to me that it would be fine fun if all of us should ride with thee, and together show ourselves in Nottingham. I would fain see what kind of fright it would give to the people."

"In good faith," cried Robin, "that would be a merry jest! And, as a good thing should be done at once, I think 'twould be better if we rode off on the errand even now."

The King nodded, and the word was given to Robin's Merry Men who were beside themselves with mirth at the thought of the joke they were about to play. And the whole goodly company, armed with their bows and arrows, set off in the direction of Nottingham town.

It was a bold and merry band! The men sang as they went, shouting out snatches of the songs of the day, such as—

"Our Robin Hood
Did what he could
Under the greenwood tree."

Or this, about the King himself:

"To the wars, one fine day
Our King went his way,
To join 'gainst the Turks in a fray—O;
But a rascally knight
Put the King in a plight,
And laid him in prison to stay—O.
      Chorus : And laid him in prison to stay—O.

And there he'd have died,
But his simple squire hied,
A-singing his songs as he went—O;
For he thought he might bawl
'Neath an old castle wall,
Where the King, himself, might be pent—O.
      Chorus : Where the King, himself, might be
            pent—O.

The thought in his mind
Was his master to find,
By humming a tune he would know—O;
So singing his song
He just jogged along
Till the King roared back with delight—O.
      Chorus : Till the King roared back with
            delight—O.

So he hastened away
For money to pay
For ransom enough to free him;
And the King came out,
And England did shout
Because it was glad to see him!
      Chorus : Because it was glad to see him!"

The King was mightily amused, and presently he said to Robin Hood:

"Why not set your men shooting, with the boughs of some distant tree as a mark, as they go on? And let the men who miss be buffetted right well by those who hit."

Robin nodded gleefully. This was a game he loved, and not only did he set the men shooting, but he raised his bow and challenged the King to do the same. Which, entering into the spirit of the thing, the King straightway did, shooting from the horse on which he rode, and Robin shooting from his, as they went on. But the King was not used to archery, except standing still and shooting at a given target, and very often he missed. But Robin rarely failed to hit. So the King did get many a buffet from Robin Hood as they went along, until his shoulders ached, and presently he cried out that the game must be stopped.

Meanwhile, the people of Nottingham, all unaware of the trick which was to be played upon them, were going about the business of their homes, and their shops, and their markets, in their usual way, until presently some on the outskirts of the town came rushing in, white with fear, to announce that Robin Hood and his Merry Men were advancing in hundreds upon the town.

"Why," they said to one another, "we thought the King was going to make an end of these men. Verily it looks as if Robin had made an end of the King. That is what must have happened, and Robin Hood and his men are coming on us in anger."

Then a panic seized the townsfolk, and each made haste to see who could be the first to flee. No one stood to face them. The men, both the Nottingham soldiers, and archers, and the labourers; the Sheriff's men, and the women and the children, and the old people, all moved along as fast as they ever could to get out of the way, until the streets were all deserted and nothing could be seen in the distance but people flying for their lives.

Oh how the King did laugh! He laughed until the tears ran down his face: but presently, when he saw the terror of his people, he sent messengers to them to tell them it was only a joke after all and it was their own King who had played it.

At first they would not believe it. They were afraid of a trap. But, at last, the King himself, simply accompanied by Robin Hood,

rode into the midst of them and allayed their
fears.

Then they crowded around their King, cheering lustily. And the King said to them:

"Ye give us good *cheers*, my merry townsfolk. But what we want is rather 'good cheer.'
We are hungry and thirsty!"

The hint was not lost upon "the good folk of
Nottingham." And it was not long before the
Cloth Hall of the town was freshly strewn with

rushes, and tables were set for the meal they were hastily getting ready. They brought in meanwhile great tankards of foaming Nottingham ales, for which the folk were famous, and the King and his knights and Robin Hood and his Merry Men did quaff them right thirstily until the tables groaned under the weight of good things, and they all sat down to eat and to drink, and then rose up to play.

But before the feast was over the King made a speech in which he told the folk of Nottingham that he had heard that Robin Hood was a bold outlaw, who cared not for his King nor his God. "That is why," said he, "I came with my followers to lay him by the heels. But, verily, sin' I have come to know him I find it was all a mistake and there are no more loyal subjects ready to fight for me and England than Robin Hood and his Merry Men. We have made an agreement together, he and I. Whatever may have been done by him in the past was done through anger at his unjust treatment by the Sheriff of this town. I will say nothing of that. I, his King, have pardoned him, and let no man ever bring it up against him any more! And on his part Robin Hood and his Merry Men have promised to come up to London and to serve me right well there. Where I go they go!—My bodyguard!"

Oh, how the people cheered! Robin—their Robin—pardoned at last, and all the men who

were with him. And now in the future they would be able to go back to their homes and look upon themselves as men who no longer need fear being taken; but go in and out like other men, no one daring to make them afraid.

There was only one thing for which they

were all sorry, and that was that they knew that, when Robin and his men went away, there were other robber bands, much more cruel and wicked, who would have them at their mercy.

However, they could only hope for the best, and Robin and his Merry Men went away with the King to the King's Court, except for some who thought it better they should stay behind. But the rest went with him. And there was silence under the greenwood tree.

TALE OF THE THREE OUTLAWS

In the day and time when Robin Hood's band separated—the master and such of his followers as chose going to the King's Court to serve the King, the rest of them returning to their own homes to live quite ordinary lives—you must not even dream there were no other bands of Merry Men like them. There were! There were several in different parts of England. So while Robin Hood settles himself down at the Court, and his men try to lead ordinary lives, we will pay a visit to the Forest of Inglewood.

Now, wherever there was forest, there were deer, and the King might pass what laws he liked, but so long as venison was such good eating, it was certain that men would kill thos. deer to turn their flesh into pasties, and cook it in various ways. It was all very well so long as they were not found out, but if they were they were outlawed like Robin Hood was, and like him they had to fly to the nearest forest.

There were three such men, called Adam Bell, Clement of the Glen, and William of Cloudesley. Outlaws were they, all three! Had they been caught, they would have been hung. So into the Forest of Inglewood they went, and in it they lived.

Now to two out of the three this did not matter the tiniest bit. They had no home and no children, so they thought it was better to live in the glorious open air, and have a time that was free from care, and make their living anywhere.

But the third man had made a chain for himself, and do what he would it tugged at his heart. He had a wife and three children in the town of Carlisle, which was quite near; so though the other two could be happy. he never could, and on one day he interrupted the whistling of the other two by springing to his feet, declaring: "It's no good! Not a bit of good! I can't rest without seeing my Alice and my three bairns. I've made up my mind to go into Carlisle, and speak with them."

The other two whistled to a different tune now. Their whistle was one of astonishment.

"If you do," said Clement of the Glen, "we'll have to go into mourning for you; for, verily, taken you will be sure to be, and if taken, hanged."

Then Adam Bell chimed in: "It's a big risk to run, friend William, just for the sake of kissing the wife and the bairns."

"Maybe," answered William. "You have neither of you ever had a wife, and neither of you ever had a bairn, or you would understand what I feel. Risk or no risk, I'm going to take it." And even as he said these words, he turned his back upon them, and swiftly they lost sight of him in the shadows of the greenwood.

Walking miles upon miles, William at last reached the outskirts of Carlisle, and found his own little cottage, and knocked at the window and called his wife. She was overjoyed to see him, and William was so taken up talking to her, that he never gave a scrap of notice to an old woman who was sitting in the corner by the kitchen hearth. Alice, his wife, had taken the old dame in, just out of sheer pity, as she had nowhere to go. But the old woman was a crosspatch, and she felt so put out that William hadn't said good evening to her, or taken a scrap of notice, that she believed he did it purposely, because he didn't want her there at all. That lit a fire in her heart, and in her head. All that Alice had done for her went for nothing at all. She only remembered the insult she believed William had put on her.

She slipped out unnoticed, and she made her way straight to the Sheriff, and said:

"Mr. Sheriff, that William of Cloudesley has come back to his home again!"

"Oh! He has, has he?" quoth the Sheriff. "Then I think I and my men will come there too." And at command from the Sheriff, his men marched after him, and over the cobbled stones of the street might have been heard the tramp, tramp, tramp of many feet.

Through the window came the sound of their tread to Alice and William. Through the window Alice and William glanced to see what it was. That one glance showed them the Sheriff and his men, and the crowd of the people behind them. William took his sword and shield, and his fine cross-bow, and he and his wife and three children went into the strongest room in the house, where the walls and the doors were stoutest. Before they did so, they shuttered the windows downstairs, and barricaded the

front door, letting down the stout oak beam
behind. This gave them a little time to make
ready to defend themselves, and suddenly a
happy thought came to Alice, and she seized
the wood chopper and took her stand inside
the front door. There she stood with the chopper raised, and behind her crouched her husband, with his cross-bow drawn ready to shoot
anyone who entered. So when the Sheriff's men
smashed in the door, this is what they saw: a
woman with a chopper, and a man with his
cross-bow.

They fell back. They knew William's skill
with that bow only too well, and it stood to
reason that it was but a piece of folly that one
or two men should die just to get the right to
make another man hang, and any one or two
of them might be the men whom William's
cross-bow slew.

But where there is a will there is a way, and
they made up their minds they would force him
to come out by setting fire to the house. Which
thing they did.

But William opened the back window, to let
his wife and three children out at the back that
way, and told them to go to the forest; and
when they were gone, William sent his arrows

flying among the crowd as long as he had any to shoot. Then, in sheer desperate spirit, he took his sword and shield, and dashed out into the crowd, smiting them as he went.

The suddenness of his attack made them all give before him; but at last, as he came into a narrow alley, a crowd massed together at the end; and those in the cottages began to throw things down upon him; and, at last, as one

struck him upon the head, he stumbled and
fell, and in a minute the crowd surged round
him like a host of wolves rushing upon a fallen
member of the pack.

He was soon bound, hand-fasted and ankle-
fasted; and once they had secured him, they
flung him into prison, there to wait until they
made him a rope-road by which to escape for
ever.

They passed the night building a scaffold
that they might hang him thereon, high up in
the sight of all men, as an object lesson to others
who might feel inclined to help themselves to
the King's deer. And the night hours sped
rapidly.

They were not the only thing which sped;
for a lad of the town, who had been out feeding
swine, heard the news on his return, and in
the darkness of the night, while they hammered
on the scaffold, he hastened to warn Adam
Bell and Clement of the Glen.

In a few hours the two outlaws were beneath
the gates of the town of Carlisle. Hearing them
knock, the porter refused to let them in. But
Clement of the Glen guessed that the porter
was an ignorant man, and showed him a letter.
At least, it looked like one; and when they

said it was a message from the King, he
was too ignorant to know better. So he
let them in, and in a trice they knocked him

down, and bound him and took away his
keys.

Up the street they dashed to where the
people were gathering to the scaffold, and they
mingled with the crowd: till, presently, the
cart in which William lay, bound hand and

foot, rumbled along the street. On the scaffold stood the Sheriff, and the chief officers of the town awaiting his arrival.

Suddenly two arrows sped swiftly through the air, and transfixed the Sheriff and one of his officers; and, as they lay there wounded and the crowd stood puzzled, his two companions dashed over to the cart, cut William's shackles free, and handed him a cross-bow and arrows to fight with them. Then the three faced the crowd, ready for business.

The good folk of Carlisle fled right and left before them, all in a panic, and when the three reached the gates, Adam Bell opened it with the keys he had stolen from the porter, and the three rushed through, locking the gate behind them, and flinging away the keys, so that their enemies were on one side and they on the other.

As they dashed onwards to the forest, they overtook a weeping woman with three weary children, who William quickly saw were Alice his wife, and his three darling bairns.

So it came to pass that afterwards they all made their home in the Forest of Inglewood, and the children grew up in the open

F

air and freedom of the greenwood shade.
And such was the fame of the shooting of
these three men that none ever dared molest
them.

ROBIN COMES BACK AGAIN

WHEN Robin Hood went up to stay at the King's Court in the City, because they liked him so much, many of his men went with him; which was what the King wanted. You see, the clever King, once he had noticed the skill of Robin Hood and his Merry Men with their bows and arrows, quickly thought to himself: "How nice it would be could I get me Robin Hood, and his skilful men, to come and live with me."

That was the thought in the King's mind. He was like a great many people. He wanted to make all he could out of others. The thought in the minds of the Merry Men, and of Robin Hood himself, was far different.

Said the Merry Men to themselves:

"If we go to the Court we shall have a place to live in. We shall have plenty of the King's beer to drink, and plenty of the King's beef to eat We have got rather tired of venison

while we have been in the Forest. Whether
it was stewed, or roasted, or boiled, or made
into pasties, venison it still was and still seemed.
In the King's Court we shall have good red
meat, and good strong ales. Then there is
another thing: we shall get regular wages from
the King; and verily we shall have a home of
our own, and can have our wives and children
with us."

The thought in the mind of Robin was:

"Until now it seems to me I have been wasting
my time. I have put right a great many things
which went wrong in Nottingham and all around.
But, after all, Nottingham is only a small place,
and the world is a very big one. Methinks I
would like to do something in the big, big
world. Who knows whether up there in London
and Winchester I may make friends amongst
the great nobles and the knights, just as I
have made a friend of the King himself. There
is noble blood in my veins, and even yet it
may be I shall be Sir Robin Hood, and by and
by, my lord the King may even let me take
up the old title which was once in our family.
There have been Earls of Chester in bygone
times in our family. It would be a fine thing
if anything I can do at Court in fighting for

the King and the country should make me
Earl of Chester again!"

So that was why Robin Hood had left
Sherwood Forest to go to the King's Court,
and that was why so many of his Merry Men
went with him.

Alack the day that Robin went! Alack the
day his men followed him! Nothing turned
out as they had hoped it would, and from the
very start everything seemed to go wrong.
Robin Hood, much to his dismay, quickly
found out when he applied for money to pay
the wages of his men, that he was expected
to pay them himself. He was told all the
nobles did it, and all the knights, and that if a
man were too poor to pay the body of men
who followed him to the wars, or, if there were
no war, drank his health in the King's Court-
yards, and the inns near by, then he had no
right to be there at all. However, Robin did
not mind much. He had brought up with him
a tremendous chest full of gold; and that was
after he had paid each of his men a share out
of the monies they had fought for and saved.
So he had plenty by him. At least, so it seemed.
He had only to go to the great chest—one of
those chests which you see in so many old

churches—very long and very deep: he had
only to go to this old chest, and look in, and
the sight of what was there seemed to say
to him:

"Don't have a worry and don't have a care,
there's money enough for you all! No matter
what you spend, nor how fast you spend it,
I shall last for many a day."

So quite lightheartedly the days passed.
When pay-day came round he was always
able to pay his men; which thing was just
what the knights and the nobles were not always
able to do. When, however, they saw that
Robin could always pay his men, they came
to him, or sent for him, and speaking to him
as if he had been their brother, they told him
how much he was liked at the King's Court. Then
they would each go on to say: "Now, Robin
Hood, I am short of money. I want to pay
my men, who are beginning to grumble. I do
not wish to borrow from the Jews. I pray
thee lend me something to go on with."

Robin Hood always did. He used to think
to himself: "Some day I may need this man
to be my friend, and support me if ever I
have to ask favours from the King, either for
myself or my Merry Men."

But this kind of thing could not go on for ever. Even that chest, which was full to the brim when he brought it, showed an astonishing amount of wood inside when he looked at it now. At first, only an inch or two of wood

made its appearance; but after several months at the Court, half the box seemed wood, and the gold was only in the other half. After a few more months, more and more of the wood was showing, and the gold only covered the bottom of the box, and presently the wood at the bottom began to show too; until there came a day at last when all Robin could see there was about a hundred coins.

Then he did a thing he had never expected to do in his life, he went to these friends of his to whom he had lent money, which had never been paid back to him, and asked them for some of it. But each of them said: "I have nothing to pay thee with!" And they seemed quite uppish and resentful because he had asked them. Then he went to other knights, and did say unto them: "I have lent me so much money in the past months, that hath never been returned, that it cometh to pass I am beginning verily to feel the want of it myself." Then he would stop, hoping, perhaps, that one of them would say, as he himself would have said, and had often said before: "Well, cheer up! Don't let that worry you! I'll lend you the money!"

But instead of that they only said in a most annoying way: "Then the more fool you!"

If it had been anywhere else but in the Court of the King, Robin Hood would have knocked them down when they spoke like this, but if anyone brawled in the King's Court, he did it knowing well that, whether he was in the right or the wrong, he would be banished from the country. And it was a good thing, too, for the Court was quite full of quarrelsome knights who were always ready to fly at one another's throats.

How Robin Hood managed after that, he never could tell. He told his men how he stood, and some of the single men stayed with him; but, of course, the married men had to slip away home; and when they got back their old habits grew too strong for them, and they made for themselves homes in the greenwood again.

Robin Hood stood it as long as he could, but one day he saw some young men of the Court practising archery with their bows and arrows, and, somehow the sight of it brought back to Robin memories of long ago.

So Robin sought out permission from the King's Chamberlain to see the King, and when it was granted, he reminded the King of a promise he had made to let him return, in case he should ever wish to. Then he went on to say there was a hunger at his heart for a sight of the old familiar scenes.

"It is a kind of homesickness which I feel, my lord the King, and until I have returned to Sherwood Forest for a time, verily I can settle down at nothing."

The King looked at him pleasantly, and said: "Verily, our word is our bond! Promised you were that you should go, if you wished, and go you shall. I will give you twice seven nights and days to go and come again, O homesick man!"

Then Robin went.

The morning he reached the Forest of Sherwood was one of the brightest mornings of the year. The sunshine had dried up the dew from the green sward, but the dew had left it all washed, and everywhere he looked he saw nothing but the soft greens he loved. Overhead the sky was deeply blue, and as he gazed he could see for many and many a mile. That is what he saw. What he heard, was this: the twitter, twitter, twitter of many a bird; and in the distance he caught the sound of a horn.

Why, it was like being at home again! The only thing wanted was a sight of his Merry Men.

So he placed his horn to his lips as in the former days, and when some of his men who were in the greenwood heard the old sound, they knew it was their master come back again, and came rushing towards him full of joy, at his return, and Robin and his Merry Men were together once more.

ROBIN HOOD IS UNHAPPY

"Robin doesn't seem himself!" quoth Little John to Will Scarlett. And when he said it he spoke the truth. He could not have said it the first day or two when Robin returned from the Court of the King, for Robin had never been more full of rough and roysterous fun: and then, quite suddenly, his behaviour had changed. He seemed to act as though he were a man who had a great trouble on his mind.

He had.

The first few days after he returned were just like a sudden holiday. When he had told the King that he felt "homesick," he had only told him the truth; and he saw how true it had been as soon as he got back into Sherwood Forest and began once more to live the old free-from-rules life. There had been so many thing one must NOT do at the King's Court; and there had been so many things one was expected to do, because everybody else did them. Here he was his own master; there, whether he liked it or not, he had—yes, simply *had* to do as others did. If he hadn't it would have made a fine confusion. But here, as I said, he was his own master.

However, when he had been back a few days, he noticed that the days were flying by. He remembered that the King had let him revisit his old haunts on the strength of his promise that he would return to the Court again in "twice seven days and nights." So as twice seven make fourteen it came about that on the morning of the eighth day Robin Hood began to get melancholy. The reason was very simple. If you had drawn near to him, as he sat over the fire at night, long after the others had gone to sleep, wrapt in his cloak, you would have heard him muttering: "I don't want to go back! I DON'T want to go back! I don't WANT to go back!" This was what was the matter with Robin, and it changed him from a man who bubbled over with fun and behaved in his old rough roystering ways, to quite another man, who strolled about by himself, and looked very unhappy, and was as peevish as a child who was sickening for something. That was why Little John had noticed the difference in him. He could not very well help it, for it was such a great difference.

The day after, Robin Hood suddenly looked up from the ground where he had flung himself in lonely mood to think, and he beckoned to Little John, Will Scarlett and Friar Tuck to come to him.

"I want you!" he said, curtly. "Sit ye down here and give me your counsel!" And, obediently, they squatted at his side.

"Now," said he. "Listen to me! It only seems yesterday since I rang my horn once again under the greenwood tree! I' faith ye were all glad to see me, but, by my word, not more glad than I was to see you all again. This!"—waving his hand to the trees of the forest—"is HOME to me! THIS is life! And to think I have got to leave it!"

"'Leave it!'" quoth Will Scarlett. "Why dost thou talk of leaving it, when thou hast only just returned?"

"Ah!" Robin replied. "I promised our gracious King to return in twice seven days and nights, and this is the tenth day. If between here and Nottingham, or, for the matter of that, between here and London, ye can find me a more miserable man than I, I very much doubt. Why, if I am to reach London on the morning of the fifteenth day, I must be off this very night."

"Then don't go!" Little John exploded. "Judging from the sorrow on thy face, thou dost not want to go."

"Thou hast said it!" answered Robin. "In very deed, I don't. But I have passed my word to the King, and, think as I will, I can see no way out. Can ye?"

They looked at one another with dismayed hearts. It certainly was a puzzle. They knew he ought to keep his word. They saw he did not want to keep it. They knew they themselves did not want him to go. When Robin was not with them, it was as though the very spring of their lives was gone. Then, at last, Will Scarlett looked at the other two, and he winked. He had seen a way out.

"We will see thee again on this matter, O Master!" he said.

"It will have to be soon then," said Robin, "for before sunset I must be on my way. Then, good-bye to this forest, good-bye to its life, good-bye to my Merry Men, and back I go to the life I hate."

It was late that afternoon. The golden sun was setting in the West, and thus far nothing had happened. Robin was sitting moodily wondering whether there really was any way out, and looked round for his Merry Men. Where was Little John? Where was Will Scarlett? Where were the rest? Where were all his Merry Men? Silently and all unnoticed they had all stolen away, and Robin, as he looked round, thought he understood. Will Scarlett, Little John and Friar Tuck had spread the news amongst them all. They had not been able to devise any means of escape, and sooner than take a sad farewell of their master they had left him to do as he pleased.

Robin understood, and sighed deeply. Then, springing to his feet, he wound his horn three times with the old familiar signal, but no one answered. Sadly, very sadly, Robin saw the truth. They had all gone away and left him to make up his own mind.

"Well," he cried, at length, "I think it is better they should take it like this! I could not bear to see their sad faces, any more than they could bear to see mine."

He gave one long, lingering glance around the old familiar glades, and muttering: "Good-

bye, Sherwood! Good-bye, happiness! Good-
bye, all that makes life worth living!" he made
his way rapidly towards the main road which
led out of the Forest.

Never a man appeared! There was not even
a sign of life. But as he was nearing the dense
bracken which hid the paths the outlaws had
made to their camp from the sight of strangers
and passers-by, there was a sound of rushing
feet, and as he turned in surprise he was roughly
seized and, in spite of his struggles, flung upon
the ground, and bound securely with ropes.

"Now," exclaimed Will Scarlett, "thou hast
often taken other men captive, thou canst
see how thou wilt like it thyself!"

It was in vain that Robin Hood protested.
Captive he was, and captive he remained.
They took away his weapons. They removed
from his pockets any knife he might have used
to set himself free. They carried him back
to his tent, and there they laid him, and took
turns to watch over him.

In the middle of the night Robin roused,
and turning to Little John enquired:

"Why hast thou done this?"

"It is the way out that thy loving companions
have hit upon. Thou art not staying of thy

own free will. Thou wouldst have kept thy word. But thou art helpless. And helpless thou wilt abide here until Will Scarlett returns from the Court and tells us how the King has taken the news."

"Thou has dishonoured me!" quoth Robin miserably.

"Nay!" said Little John. "Thou art not staying here of thine own free will. Thou art a captive. The King himself knows what it

is to be taken captive and held against his
will, so he will understand. Rest content, O
Master, and wait for the return of our
messenger!"

Content or not, there Robin had to stay.
Four days and nights went by ere Will Scarlett
reached the Court of the King, and was ushered
into the King's presence.

Humbly bending upon his knee, the great,
lumbering fellow told his tale: the tale of a
sorrowing man who had tried to keep his
word unto the King, and was held captive
against his will. And as the King listened he
bit his lips in sheer vexation.

"Ye say he was anxious to come?" he
questioned, fiercely.

"He was, my Lord King! But we were more
anxious to keep him. In the Forest he is like
a fine picture in its proper frame; but on thy
Court, O King, there is nothing fine either in
the picture nor in the frame. They do not suit
one another. Let him remain, and we all of
us will be thy servants for ever in every troublous
time that may come to thee, but if thou take
him from us, then, verily, I think he will be
Robin Hood without his Merry Men."

"And thou sayest he is held prisoner by his

own men? Whoever heard the like of it? Get
ye back, and tell Robin Hood that in payment
for his living in my Forest, I shall demand a
fee, and the fee will be his service, and the

service of his Merry Men in case I ever need
ye; and God knows it may be very soon!"

So Will Scarlett returned, and in another
four days and nights he reappeared in the
Forest. Then with his knife he severed the
bonds of Robin Hood, and told his tale.

And Robin accepted the King's terms, and for a score more of years he and his men lived on in the Forest, and the story of what they did has yet to be told you.

ROBIN HOOD GOES INTO TRADE

It fell upon a day as Robin Hood was taking one of his strolls that he met one of the villagers jogging along in his cart; and that it was a butcher's cart was plain to see, for it was filled with meat he was hurrying to the Market in Nottingham to sell.

Now, when Robin saw him, an imp of mischief entered his mind, and swift as a flash of lightning he saw a way to carry out a fine plan, which was full of promise of a new adventure of quite another kind from any he had had as yet. So he hailed the man and for a time he walked beside the cart.

"I see thou has a fine lot of meat in thy cart!" he said. "And the head of thy horse is set as though thou wouldst go to Nottingham."

"It is to Nottingham that I am bound," agreed the other. "And it is a far journey; but there is no other market which is more nigh. I only wish there were!"

"There is," said Robin gravely. "I know of one, which will take not only all thou hast there but all thou canst provide of meat for the next few weeks. But it will depend upon thy price. What wast thou to get for thy meat in Nottingham town, if that is, thou didst sell it all?"

"The meat would bring me in, if I sold it all, two and a half marks; and thou canst have it and more like it at that price, and welcome."

"But," said Robin, "I should want to buy thy mare, as well as thy meat, and if I throw in another one and a half marks for mare and cart, wilt thou sell me all for four marks, and any more meat I may want at the same price as the meat in thy cart?"

So, overjoyed that he need not make the long journey to Nottingham, the butcher let him have the meat and the mare and the cart, and Robin also bought from him the butcher's smock which he wore; and away the man went.

Robin drove the cart straight into the camp and, first having got rid of his Lincoln green, he was soon driving himself to Nottingham to the stalls in the Market Place where he hoped to sell the meat. He went first of all to the

Sheriff and paid the market dues without which none could sell and then took up his stand with the rest and offered his meat to the folk who wished to buy.

At first, as he seemed a stranger, no one came, but when the rest glanced at him and heard him crying his meat at a price which was five times cheaper than any of the other butchers, they thought at first he was merely joking.

Joking! It may have seemed so to them, and in the beginning Robin had only meant his butcher's prank for a joke. It was only when he saw the high price the other butchers were charging for their meat that he made up his mind to teach them a lesson. "Why," he thought, "should these tradesmen drag money, and make big profits, out of the poor folk of Nottingham?" This was why he was selling his meat five times as cheaply as the others.

The folk smiled, and at first they passed on, but at last one good woman bought some, and in her triumph she went round the market showing what she had bought. In a few minutes Robin was as busy as could be. In another few minutes the crowd were hustling and jostling to get to his stall while the spaces in front of the other stalls grew empty.

The other butchers could not help noticing it, and when they found out why it was they were furious, and could come only to the conclusion that he was silly and daft. So they determined to have some fun with him.

Immediately business was over they pretended to be very friendly, and invited him down to the inn to drink with them, as everyone did in those days.

Nothing loath, Robin went along with them, and when they had had one round of drink, he called for some more, and yet for some more, and paid the reckoning each time. Then, at last, he invited them to a feast, and the innkeeper had hard work to do to provide them sufficient fare. Then, while Robin Hood was fumbling about in the pocket of his butcher's smock for the money to pay with, they began to whisper to one another:

"This man spends money like water! I shouldn't be surprised if he has been selling some of his land, and having got the money is squandering it in this fashion."

"Yes," said another. "That is what it means, or else, as I said before, the stranger is just daft."

Now, while all this had been going on, the Sheriff himself had come in and sat down with the rest. Anyone in those days, be he squire or parson or sheriff, or soldier, or farmer, mingled freely with the rest in any inn. So seeing the impression Robin had made on the others, and believing as they did that Robin was daft, he made up his mind to get what he could out of him.

"Thou must have plenty of cattle of thine own to be able to sell it at such a price in the form of meat," remarked the Sheriff to Robin. And when he heard him speak thus Robin's eyes twinkled with mischief, and he replied:

"I have indeed so many that I should like to sell some."

The Sheriff winked at the others, and then he gravely proposed to Robin to sell some of them to him, and Robin agreed, saying that he had some two or three hundred head of cattle on his farm in the country not far away.

"An' that be so," quoth the Sheriff, "thou must have much land on which they graze. Perhaps as thou art selling the beasts, thou wouldst like to part with some of thy land?"

"Ay, ay! That I would," said the seemingly silly man. "I have a hundred or so acres of good pasture land, and I will sell it to thee cheap."

"But what about the title to it?" asked the Sheriff.

"Oh, I'll give you as good a title to it as ever my father gave to me. Come and see it, an' if thou likest it, thou canst buy it for three hundred pounds in gold."

It seemed like a bargain, so the Sheriff rose, saddled his good steed, put three hundred pounds in gold into a bag, and away he went, Robin Hood jogging along in his cart and the Sheriff ambling beside him.

In course of time they drew near to the Forest, and suddenly the Sheriff much amused Robin by saying: "I trust that whatever may happen we may not meet with a man they call Robin Hood! May God save us from meeting him this day! Otherwise thou wouldst never get thy price for either farm or beast!"

Presently they rode into the midst of the Forest, and suddenly they saw, as they glanced through a clearing, a hundred head of good red deer, tripping along.

Then Robin turned to the Sheriff, and with a wave of his hand, said, "These are my horned beasts, good Sheriff! I trow they are fat and

sleek enough for thee!" And as he spoke he
pulled from under his blouse his trusty horn,
and blew three blasts upon it, and out there
tumbled, from every side, a company of his
Merry Men.

Then Robin took hold of the Sheriff's horse,
and tied it fast to a tree, while the Sheriff
stood there trembling. They stripped his mantle
from off his back, and spread it upon the ground,
and out of the Sheriff's side-pocket deep they
fetched that three hundred pounds.

"Thou didst set a trap for me," quoth Robin, "but thou hast fallen into it thyself. Thou mayest go—yea, back to thy home, but before we let thee depart all safe and sound, I want thee to sing to my Merry Men the song you sang to me in the inn."

And the Sheriff he sang in trembling tones, and then he was set scot-free. They placed him once more on his ambling steed, with his face to the tail, and gave him the tail to hold; and away the steed trotted towards the town, and not till he reached it could the Sheriff get down.

The people crowded around him, wondering what thing had happened unto their Sheriff. And it was with shame of face and heart he told them. Then, like a man who has done a silly thing and seeks to lay the blame upon others, he turned furiously upon the butchers, and said:

"Ye stand there laughing at me now, but had ye not been laughing at him then, never should I have thought him a feckless fool, and believed I could drive a good bargain with him for myself. Now must I hie me home with my good three hundred pounds gone. And what shall I say to my mistress?"

There was silence for a minute; for they all knew that the wife of the Sheriff was a woman with a bitter tongue, and then the Vicar of one of the Nottingham churches, who was in the crowd, said gravely:

"Nay, Master Sheriff, that is not the question! The question is, What will she say to thee?"

Ah!—It was! And it was not long before the Sheriff found it out. Long and bitter were her complainings. For three hundred pounds in those days were worth three times what they are worth to-day. It had meant a lot of scheming to get them, either to save or spend, and now they had vanished. No wonder she was bitter!

SPITE AND RESPITE

You may imagine that when the Sheriff had told his tale to his shrew of a wife, she said some bitter things to him. No, she did not say them all at once: she kept on flinging the thing up at him. Every fresh thing he tried to do in making a bargain with any other man, she would sneer: "Are you sure he is not another Robin Hood?" Sometimes, when he grew angry with her himself about any other matter, and said impatiently, as husbands in those days did to their wives: "Hold thy tongue!" and, "Woman, be not a fool!" she would answer: "Ask the townsfolk which of the two of us is the fool?"

It was very hard to put up with: but she had the best of it in every way, and at last one night, just after he had refused her a new dress, saying: "I cannot afford it, Mistress!" she had snapped back: "Nay, thy good money has gone to dress Robin Hood and his Merry Men!"

After that she would not lie down, and she would not be quiet. She was wound up and scolded on until her husband wanted to smack her; but suddenly in her rage she said a thing which set him thinking.

This was it:

"If any other man but thyself were Sheriff, he would try to take Robin Hood. If he couldn't get Robin Hood, he would take some one else who had long bows hidden in their homes like Robin Hood's Merry Men. There must be many of them about. Then thou couldst hang them by the neck, and Robin Hood and his men would have a lesson which would make them pause. But thou art a do-nothing! A good-for-nothing! Was there ever a poor woman who had such a feckless fool for a husband as I have!"

Now there is one thing that being a Sheriff gave a man a right to do in those days. He had the right to command his men to enter into any house and search it. So when his wife scolded the Sheriff in this fashion, what she said gave him an idea. There was something in what she said, after all. He could not seize

G

Robin Hood, but he might stab him in the back by taking it out of some other fellows. He knew how bitterly Robin would feel it.

So the next morning, for the first time for many weeks, the Sheriff got up whistling. He saw a way to revenge himself upon Robin Hood. He called the Sheriff's officers and told them to take a party of men, and to search all the cottages which were on the edge of Sherwood Forest, on the Nottingham side of the Forest.

"If," said he, "ye find any long bows in the cottages, then do ye at once arrest the men who own them, and bring them along to me. I will deal with them. Unless men are the King's archers, it is only reasonable to believe that if they live on the edge of the Forest, and they have long bows in their homes, then they use them on the King's deer."

Away went the Sheriff's men, bent upon their errand. It was just the errand they liked. They entered home after home, but never a long bow did they find, and it looked as if they would go back empty-handed; but last of all they entered the cottage of a poor widow, who had three sons, and in that cottage they found three long bows. That night, when the

Sheriff's men returned to Nottingham, there were three young men who marched with them to be tried, and they were the three sons of the widow.

"But," I think I hear some of you say, "these men had nothing to fear. No one had caught them using their bows to kill the King's deer! So what could they have against them?"

Ah, the Sheriff saw to that. He went and saw the magistrates: he was one of the magistrates himself, and they were all his friends. So when the men were brought up to be tried, he knew how things would be decided, and to make quite sure he also saw to it that the jury was made up of men who had promised to do as he wished. Of course, the three sons of the widow were found guilty and they were sentenced to be hanged.

Now in the court, when the sentence was pronounced, there stood up an old man with a robe which was tattered and torn, and who leaned heavily upon his staff. The robe was the robe of one of those pilgrims, called a palmer, who had been all the way over sea and over land, to the Holy Land with the Crusaders; and because he was a holy man and a kind of priest, they listened to what he had to say with respect. He pleaded for the young men, but he pleaded in vain. Then said he: "I will shake off the dust of my feet from this town, for it is a wicked and unjust place; I will leave it to-morrow morn."

It was the glorious month of May. The morning sun was shining brightly through the green trees of the Forest when, quite early, Robin Hood rode out towards Nottingham to see what and whom he could meet. For very joy of heart he was singing to himself about the "Merry, merry month of May," when suddenly, as he neared the town, he saw a wretched old woman sitting by the door of her cottage, evidently in great grief.

An old woman!—An old woman who was in trouble! Robin could never pass her by! If ever he saw a child or a woman or an old person in trouble, it made Robin feel as if he could cry himself. So he got off his horse, and when he asked her what was the matter, he heard the story of the Sheriff's cruel treatment of her three sons.

In a moment Robin saw the spite and malice which was in the Sheriff's heart. Those three sons were being killed to give him and his

Merry Men a lesson. Anger flamed in his heart.

"Verily," he muttered to himself, "I will teach this Sheriff another lesson!"

Then he turned to the widow, and told her to dry her eyes; for he himself would go to Nottingham and see what could be done.

Away he rode, and on the main road he met the palmer who was keeping his word, and

shaking off the dust of his feet from the wicked
town.

When Robin saw him he got off his horse,
and knelt to the holy man, and the holy man
blessed him.

Presently he told Robin he was leaving the
town because these three young men were condemned to be hanged in the public field at
noon that very day.

"O holy palmer!" cried Robin, "thou canst
help me save them. All that thou needst to
do is to lend me thy palmer's robe, all tattered
and torn, and put on my clothes of Lincoln
green. Besides which I will give thee forty
silver shillings for the use of thy garments."
And the old man did so.

It took some time to make the exchange,
for it was a trouble for the palmer to get into
Robin's clothes, more than it was for Robin
to get into his; but at last it was done, and then
Robin set off for Nottingham, leaning upon
his staff, and creeping along like an old, old
man.

Now it had come to pass that the feeling
in the town ran high about this very thing.
Men who had listened to the trial saw there
was something strange about it, and the folk

had been standing at the doors of their houses whispering all the morning; and above all things which had moved them was the way in which the holy palmer had pleaded for them in court with the cruel Sheriff.

Suddenly he caught sight of the palmer, and striding up to him, he said, sneeringly:

"So you have come back again, after all!"

"Yes," said the palmer humbly. "I felt it did not beseem me to turn my back upon those three young men. I would have thy permission to be to them their father confessor, and give them pardon for whatever evils they may have done."

So, because he thought it would please the mutinous people, the Sheriff did not refuse him the privilege, and the pretended palmer was taken to the cell of the three condemned men.

What he did there, and whether he succeeded in setting them free, belongs to the next part of the story.

But the crowds of people who were coming into the town for the execution did not know that, and the crowds of the people who were gathered at their doors still went on murmuring as well they might; and when they saw the holy palmer walking with the Sheriff with slow and painful steps they made up their minds that something was happening, in which the holy man was taking part. Oh, if they had known the truth!

Over and over again Robin Hood had great work not to laugh aloud, as he realised how completely his disguise had taken them all in. But he kept it back and, as he reached the cells, he began to mutter as though he were muttering the prayers of a man like himself; and when the men saw him and heard him say to them:

"My sons, I have come to prepare you for your forthcoming trial, and to help you," they fell on their knees.

ROBIN HOOD SAVES THE
THREE MEN

I HAVE told you that when Robin Hood entered
the cell, where the three men were spending
their last hours, the moment the men saw
him dressed as a holy palmer they fell on their
knees. Their hands were already tied behind
them, so that it was rather awkward; but none
the less Robin prepared to receive their confessions.

The surly gaoler stood at the door of the tiny
cell, which really was only large enough for
one, but had been made to hold the three
prisoners, and Robin Hood turned on him
saying, with fire flashing from his eyes:

"I have come here to give these poor men
my blessing and to hear the last things they
wish to say. But, unless thou dost wish me
to curse thee at the same time, take thyself,
and that quickly, out of our hearing! It is
not meet that anyone but myself should listen
to their last words."

This was enough for the gaoler, and he darted away as if he had been stung, which was just what Robin wished. Then he turned to the three men and began to speak.

What Robin seemed to say was a continued sound of muttering as though he were a priest mumbling prayers. What he actually did say was this:

"Listen! Listen with all your ears! Obey what I say to you! Obey what I say to you!" he muttered in low tones. "I am going to cut your cords and leave you free! I have come from your mother. Do you understand?"

"Yea, Father, I understand."

"Then I will come back to you in one moment, when I have finished with your brothers!"

On he went to each of them in turn and said the same thing. And they murmured their reply; whereupon he glided behind them and swiftly cut the knot which bound their hands so that one tug of theirs could break them loose. Then he said: "Ye will have to march through the town in the procession to the field where ye are to be executed, and I will march with you, motioning the people back. Listen with all your ears until I say the word 'NOW!' Then tug at your knot and run for your lives!

If I mistake not they will be so surprised that
ye will be out of the field before the Sheriff
and his men comprehend what has happened.
The people are all in your favour, and they will
get in the way once the Sheriff's men begin to
pursue. Do ye understand?" And the men,
with their hearts beating wildly at the thought
of escape, answered humbly that they did.

All this was carried on in the low tones in
which the ministers of Holy Church talk to
their penitents, and when Robin had finished
hearing their supposed confessions, he stood at
the doorway and muttered words which were
intended to sound like a prayer: though it was
only a mumble-jumble of some stray words of
Latin which Robin had picked up.

Having done this he went to the door and
announced that they were all ready, and as it
was nigh noon the Sheriff's men formed up
outside the gaol, walking in front, and the three
men fell into the procession with bowed heads,
doing their best to obey Robin Hood, who
whispered to them as they came out of the
door: "Look as if ye were half dead with fright,
men!"

Verily they did! They kept their eyes on
the ground as though they were ashamed to be

seen. They walked as slowly as though they scarce could drag one leg before the other through craven fear; and Robin came behind muttering to himself, as though he were the holy palmer himself. On the right hand rode the Sheriff dressed in his best, as though it were a holiday, and his heart was full of spite and malice and pride; for he was thinking to himself:

"This will be a fine lesson to Robin Hood and his Merry Men. If anything will strike fear into their hearts, it will be this!"

They walked onward towards the Town gate and the fields where the gallows had already been built, which were full of people. But before they reached this open space they had to pass the Sheriff's house, and there at the window was seated his proud wife, who had suggested this plan to her husband. She looked down upon the throng with bitter scorn upon her face, and the folk who saw her whispered to each other: "Doesn't she just wish that it was Robin Hood, Little John, and Will Scarlett walking there instead of them!"

She did indeed: but since she could not get Robin Hood and his men, she was glad that these three were going to their doom. Never a thought of sorrow for the old widow who would lose her three sons crossed her mind, nor the mind of her husband.

The people, however, kept murmuring aloud at the cruel injustice of the thing. Some of them booed the Sheriff and his men. They pressed closer and closer, so that at one time it looked as if they would hinder the progress of the procession. But Robin motioned them back and they made way.

There, at last, they stood at the foot of the gallows and a great hush fell upon the crowd. The fateful moment had come, and very soon they expected to see these three fine young fellows dangling in the air.

But Robin drew near to them again as if he would whisper a parting blessing. Then he stood back from them and they waited with heads bowed until Robin said to the people: "Everything is now ready!" And turning to the Sheriff's men, he cried: "Do your worst." And then he shrieked: "NOW!"

The moment they heard this word the three young men sprang forward as if they were running a race, and the ropes which had bound their hands fell from behind them on to the ground. Moved by a sudden impulse the crowd

cleared away and Robin tore after them in his
pilgrim's cloak.

It had all turned out just exactly as Robin
expected. The Sheriff and his men were so

taken by surprise that for quite a space they
stood stock-still and made no attempt either to
run after them or to shoot with their arrows.
And, as Robin had foreseen, once the good
folk realised that the three men were trying to

escape, they broke up in confusion and hindered the Sheriff's officers, who were afraid to shoot in case they hurt some of the people.

The Sheriff's men grew crimson with rage and beat back the people with their staves, and as soon as a lane had been formed by their efforts they began fitting arrows to their bows so as to shoot the escaped men. But by this time Robin Hood had gained the shelter of the woods, and standing back behind a tree he called out:

"Back, I say!—Back! if ye value your lives! The first who dares move an inch nearer or tries to shoot shall die by my hand!"

Then, as the crowd waited, Robin's voice rang towards them:

"It is Robin Hood speaking!"

And when the people heard that, they shouted themselves hoarse, while the Sheriff called hastily to his men: "Go ye and get him!"

But they never budged! And Robin, hurrying from tree to tree, got further and further back into the forest. Presently from a distance they heard the sound of a horn, and they jumped at once to the belief that Robin was back within the Forest.

Then the crowd broke up! The men went

home and told their wives what had happened,
and their old mothers, as they crouched in the
chimney corners, murmured:

"A very good thing for the widow, too! How

should I like to have lost three manly sons,
and on the gallows, too! God bless her and
may the saints protect them!"

That was the way most of the people looked
at it. In their hearts they were right glad that

the lads had escaped. But there was one home in that town where there was a terrible storm of temper. I needn't tell you it was the Sheriff's house, and that the sound of the storm was caused by the angry words which the wrathful Sheriff's wife was letting fly at her husband's head.

Oh, how she stormed! There was scarcely a word, a really nasty word, in the English language which she didn't use.

Many were the people whom the Sheriff had made suffer! But he got it all back again from his wife, and he determined he would never leave a stone unturned until he had laid that Robin Hood by the heels.

But, meanwhile, the three men went into safety and they joined the band of the Merry Men and became some of its most useful members. They would have laid down their lives for Robin, who had saved them from the gallows!—but then, they would all of them have done that!

ROBIN HOOD AND THE HONEST PINDER

In the olden days when Robin Hood lived there were a good many unjust laws, as you can see by some of the old stories. However, they were not all unjust. Some of them were wise and necessary, and one of these necessary rules which was at work all through the country was the law about stray cattle.

Cattle, whether they are sheep, or oxen, or bulls, or pigs, or animals such as donkeys or horses, have a rare trick of getting out from the place where they ought to be, and finding their way where they ought not to be. In those days the trick was easy to work, for such hedges as there were were only made of small bushes, or else of stone. Any curious cow could easily get through by forcing its way through the bushes. The other cattle could break out of the farm-yard, and the horses and donkeys could easily leap anything. This made a great danger at

night. The roads were always bad enough, but
when to this you had to add the chance of
running into stray animals—well, it made things
very awkward.

That was why every town and city and little
market town had a small field all fenced around
into which they turned any stray animals
which might be caught on the highway. They
called it the "pound"; and once there, there
the cattle or horse or donkey had to stay.
If the owner missed them he would make
enquiries, and when he found them he had to
pay for all it had cost to keep the animals, and
he also had to pay a fine for the damage they
had done or might have done in their wander-
ings.

Ah, but who did the catching? Who turned
them into the "pound" when they were caught?
Who took the money from the owners? And
who made them pay it before the animals were
allowed to go? Why, "the pounder," as they
called the man who had charge of the place.
By degrees the word "pounder" got turned into
"pinder," just as the word "bounder," a man
who bound books, became "binder." Little by
little each of these men became known as "the
pinder."

Yes, it was a very necessary rule, but it depended on the pinder how it worked out. If he were a nice kind of man he soon let people know when he had got one of their animals. If he were a nasty kind of man, he didn't, and as the longer they stayed the bigger the pay, it fell rather hard on the owners when they stayed too long.

Being a pinder was a jolly sort of a job. There was no real hard work, and there was usually a snug little cottage put there for the pinder with plenty of ground for garden, and for keeping hens, and chickens, and pigs, and a piece of common for his own animals to feed upon. So men were glad to get these posts; but as these posts were generally given by the Lord of the Manor, or one of the nobles, it stands to reason that the man who hoped to be a pinder, or to keep the place once he had got it, had to keep in with the gentry who put him there.

This tale is about a pinder who lived in a district called Wakefield. He had been there ever so long, and he become known everywhere as the "honest pinder." The reason for this was that he never made any difference between the animals of the poor and the rich. The owner might be Lord of the Manor, or a Squire,

or a Noble, or he might be just a poor Peasant.
It didn't matter! If those animals were caught
straying, then Lord or Squire, or Noble or
Peasant, he had to pay the fine.

This pinder cared for no man. The only
thing he cared for was to do his job. He stood
up to Lord, and Squire, and Noble. He had
stood up for friend and foe. He took no less
from any man than was his right, and he took
no more. Little by little people found it out,
and admired him for his pluck. Presently,
finding he could be trusted, they made him
Highway Officer too; that is, the man who, if
he caught men trespassing in the corn fields,
could make them to pay for their trespass just
as he made the owners of straying cattle. No
matter who they were the pinder saw to it that
pay they did!

That was how he came into the lives of Robin
Hood, Will Scarlett, and Little John. They
had walked many and many a long mile from
Sherwood Forest over the borders of Nottingham, into Yorkshire. They loved these long
walks and the adventures they met with while
they were on their journey. Little they cared
for rules about highways, or rules of any kind.
If they wanted to go anywhere they took the

shortest cut they could find, instead of sticking
to the high roads. Through the cornfields or
any other fields they made their way. They
always had, and men were so afraid of the three

broad-shouldered men when they were together
that they winked at what they did.

It fell upon a day that they came near the
town of Wakefield. In order to reach the town
they cut straight across some fields which were

waving with golden corn. They were laughing and chatting with themselves, when suddenly, as they came out of the field, they heard a blustering voice crying:

"What are you varlets doing there? Can't you see the difference between the King's highway and a field, you simpletons?"

Robin Hood looked round in astonishment. He was not used to being spoken to in this way, and then he saw, by the gate which led out of the field into the highway, a great broadshouldered, burly man. It was the honest pinder of Wakefield.

"Do you know whom I am?" queried Robin, laughing.

"I neither know nor care! Who you may be matters not. What does matter is I am set here to see folk do not stray out of the highway into fields, or if they do to make them pay!"

Robin winked at his two companions.

"'Make them pay!'" quoth Robin. "That is easy to say, but how wilt thou do it? We are three to one!"

"Ye might be thirty to one for aught I care," the pinder replied sturdily. "I have a good staff in my hand which I can wield on the head of any man, or any men, who try to cross a field. So, my good fellow, though you have swords and I only have my staff, you'll have to fight your way, or each of you must pay."

He leaned his back against a tree close by the stile, and planted his foot the other side of the stile, and raised his staff.

"Here's a pretty play!" cried Robin, and rushed for him with his drawn sword. But the eye of the pinder was swift, and the skill of his hand was cunning, and the strength of his arm was great, and ere Robin could leap the stile to use his sword, he found his sword-arm almost broken. Then Will Scarlett leapt into the fray. But he shared the same fate. Then Little John tried his hand, but his sword was no sooner drawn than it was knocked out of his grasp, and the very blade broken.

So they went at it for the best part of an hour. Had it been in the field they might have surrounded him, but there was only room for one at the time across that stile, and when the three tried to rush it together, he sent his staff whirling round.

Now if there was one thing Robin Hood admired it was pluck. So at length he ceased the struggle, and paid his trespass fee right generously. Then he said to the pinder:

"I think I can find thee a merrier job than doing such work as this. Why not be one of

my Merry Men, and live in the green wood with me?"

The pinder shook his head. "I am bound to my master for three months more, till Michaelmas next is o'er. I'd join to-day, but

that's not my way! I have passed my word
for a year to the day, and here to the day I will
stay! Were it not for this I'd come with thee
now, for my master and I've had a row. His
beasts are clapt in the town, and he fain would
get them out without the poundage fee. But
though he were Lord, or Noble, or Squire, that
thing should never be, but my word has been
passed, so here I'm held fast, till three months
have come and have gone. But when Michaelmas comes and I've gathered my fee, then I'll
set as little store by him as my master sets store
by me! I'll take my bow and staff in my hand,
and come to the green wood to thee."

It was in vain Robin urged him. He only
shook his head!

"Under the green wood I'll meet thee after
Michaelmas."

This is the story of how the honest pinder of
Wakefield joined the band of Robin Hood and
his Merry Men; for he kept his word, and
when Michaelmas was over another pinder
stood in his place, and he had gone to the
Forest.

But when he came it was still as the sturdy
honest man! If there was any adventure that
Robin undertook, to put right anything which

had gone wrong, he could always rely on the pinder. But if anything were planned which seemed to him unjust, then would he have nought to do with it. Honest he was, and honest he stayed!

THE BITERS BIT

ROBIN HOOD, Little John, and Will Scarlett were not the only men in the band who loved to go out in search of adventure. Yes, when times were dull and they were not under the orders of Robin to take part in an attack all together, others often stole away to see what they could happen upon by themselves.

It was just on such an occasion as this that three of the youngest members of the band made up their minds to see what they could turn up in the way of fun. They wanted to do something highly original. They had talked it over the night before and one of them had said:

"Why not take our bows and arrows and pretend that we are only new hands at the game, and come back laden with prizes?"

"What!" exclaimed another of the three. "That's only an old trick of Robin's and Little John's. Everybody's awake to it by now. No, that would be a stale joke!"

The other frowned. "It's all very well for you to sit there and say what is stale," he replied. "But tell us something fresh!"

Challenged in this fashion, the man puckered up his brows, thinking hard. Then at last he said:

"I tell ye a good idea. Let's go and pretend to be out of work. Three young men, who want to work badly! And because we can't we are driven to beg from the passers-by."

"All very well," grumbled the one who hadn't spoken yet. "But what shall we do if a man to whom we tell that tale offers us work to do?"

"Well, we should have to do it, that's all!" said the other. "And there's one comfort, the job wouldn't last long. Let's go off early in the morn and see how much money we can make at the game."

This was why they got up extra early in the morning so that all three could get away without being observed. At least they thought they would. But it was no good; for that Little John was sitting there, whittling sticks! He always was up with the sunrise and began to gape like the birds as soon as it went down. He smiled when he saw them.

"Hullo," he cried, "off on adventure bound? What is it to-day?"

"Begging!" they cried in chorus.

"And who, think ye, will give to ye?" he smiled. "And if ye came to me to beg, verily I would look at ye and say: 'Ye are young! And youth should be strong. Strong enough to work. Ye are lazy, yea, ye are lazy!'— THAT is what I would say to ye. And so will others." And he lay back and laughed heartily.

"Well, Little John, ye may be a true prophet, but anyway we are going out to see," answered one. And they stepped out blithely, leaving Little John rolling on the greensward for very mirth.

However, it was even as Little John said. Men and women alike scorned their tale. Some would not even stop to listen! Those who did would not believe. Some even said plainly to their faces that there must be something very wrong with three stalwart lads, if they had to stoop to beg their way and owe their meals to others. "If ye cannot do otherwise," said one, "go and offer yourselves as soldiers for the country!"

As night came on apace they had to sleep under the hedges, and a storm came on and burst over their heads and they were soaked through and through. So the three Merry Men who had started out so blithely, faced the next morning with grumpy hearts at the way things had turned out for them. They began to see that a beggar's life was not so easy as it seemed.

There was one thing, however, in the draggled condition that they were, all of them looked so wretched that a good woman gave them some ale and beef for breakfast; but even she scolded all the time; and they were glad to get away on their journey through the slushy roads.

In the midst of it out came the sun. It shone brightly and hotly, and under its kiss the roads began to dry. Their garments did the same, and presently they began to pluck up heart and hoped that the second day would be better than the first. They hoped it all the morning; they hoped it all the afternoon, but no one came their way to beg from and at last their hope died in their hearts.

Then, just as they were thinking of going out of business, they saw riding slowly down the road a man who had hanging from each side of his nag a long sack.

They gave a shrewd guess and whispered to each other: "It is a miller. He has been to the mill to get some grist ground into flour and he is bringing the flour back."

Their guess was all right; for as he approached they saw that he was dusty with the powder of the mills and even his face was white with it.

He was no sooner near them than they began to beg with all their might. They asked for money to get a night's lodging and a bit of food. But the miller rode along steadily, and they might have been talking to a deaf man for all the notice he gave them. They ran alongside, but he did not look down either to the right nor to the left but straight before him, just as if at both sides of him there were not these pestilent, muttering beggars, trying to tell him their tale of woe. So on he rode, trip-a-trip, trip-a-trip! He might have had no eyes in his head, and no voice wherewith to speak, for he made no sound and seemed as though he did not even see them.

This was too much for their patience. One of them seized the bridle and stopped the nag and the others tumbled him off his horse and set upon him. "Now," they said breathlessly, after the struggle; for struggle it had been. The miller was a burly man and a bit of a wrestler, and they had hard work to get him upon the ground and keep him there. "Now," they said, "what thou wouldst not give us we will take. Where is thy money?"

"I have none with me," he cried. But as they disbelieved him they went over his pockets, but there was nothing in them except his hand-kerchief and plenty of flour powder from the mill.

"It is no good looking there," he said at last. "If you want to get at my money you must get it at the bottom of the sacks. That is where it all is. If you will set me free, I will get it for you."

Laughing, they let him get up, and then as he went to the bags they kept quite near him while he took down one of the sacks from the saddle. He placed it upon the ground and reached his arm far into it as though to reach the money, but when he withdrew his arm his hand was full of flour, and quick as thinking he flung it into the eyes and face of the man nearest to him; once more he dipped and did the same thing, and while they spluttered blindly in their surprise he jumped upon the nag and for once made her go quickly. But before he tore off out of sight he left them a parting gift in the shape of a blow upon the head of each with his staff which well-nigh stunned them.

"Ha, hah!" he cried. "How like ye my money?" But they could not answer, for he was swiftly out of sight.

"So this is the life of a beggar," quoth one. "It liketh me not."

"NOR ME!" cried the other two.

"Two days have we been at it. Nearly two whole days! And for our pains we have had nothing but a drenching night, a breakfast from a scold, and a handful of flour flung

into our eyes. The world is a stingy world, my brothers."

And the brothers answered: "Even so!"

But even as they spoke the rain came down again, and once more before they could brush

the signs of that flour away they found it
damped into a paste—a paste that nothing
could remove. So just as they were they
tramped back to the camp wearily, the camp
they had left so gleefully, and no sooner after
their long journey had they entered it than
Little John caught sight of them and roared
with laughter again. Hearing his mirth the
men gathered round and Robin Hood himself
drew near.

Little by little they drew the story out of
them; and that they spoke truth was clear from
the flour upon their clothes. So when the band
heard it they were for going after that miller
and punishing him; but the Honest Pinder got
upon his feet and said: "It served them right.
If an honest miller can't go to and fro between
his work without being robbed by men of this
band it is a fine look out. Had I been there
it would have been his part and not yours I
should have taken. Flour in your eyes, indeed.
It ought to have been pepper! What kind of
scandal do you think will be set going about
us now? I know what folk will say! They
will say, 'Well, if that is the sort of thing
Robin's men will do—WELL!'"

The others began to murmur, but Robin

cried: "He is right! To-morrow, ye shall send down to the miller and pay him for the flour which was spilt; and tell him that the whole thing was but a joke."

And as he said so was it done!

TWO CHUMS FALL OUT

THERE were one or two drawbacks to being in the Forest! One was that it was difficult to get a doctor when you were ill; but by long practice most of the men had become skilled in dealing with broken bones, sprained ankles, wounds, and colds and coughs. It may sound strange to you, but there, there in the open air, they had very few colds, and very rarely heard a cough. That was one drawback, but another was that they were ever so far away from a church. Sometimes, as the sound of church bells was carried by the wind to the camp, some of the men would sigh.

Robin himself was like this, and one day he startled Little John by declaring: "I am going to Nottingham. I am going there to church!"

He said this in the hearing of several of the men, and they offered to go with him, so that if he were discovered they could surround him, and bring him home safely. But Robin roughly refused, saying:

"Verily, I will go alone! An' if anyone goes with me it shall be Little John."

So the two went together. But on the way it seemed that Robin was in a funny, quarrelsome mood. Everything Little John said Robin contradicted. This kind of thing is catching, so presently, everything Robin said, Little John contradicted too.

This went on for a mile or two: then, at last, their wordy war came to an open quarrel. Robin Hood lost his temper, and quite suddenly he turned and struck Little John. They glared at one another for a moment: then, Little John laid his right hand upon the hilt of his sword, and he growled:

"If thou wert not the leader of our band, thou shouldst pay for that rough blow. As it is, and because thou art unarmed thyself, I will take it from thee! But verily, I will not risk another. Thou art my master no more. Thou mayest get another in my place from to-day. I have done with thee!"

There was a sound of crunching of bracken beneath the feet of Little John as he turned in his wrath out from the highway into the Forest, and Robin was left alone.

Robin continued his journey into Nottingham, more angry than ever because Little John had left him. But there is nothing drives away anger better than a long walk, so by the time Robin reached Nottingham he felt quite sorry and ashamed of himself.

He went into a church in Nottingham, and knelt down, and it was while he was kneeling in this church that one of the monks caught sight of his face, and knew him in an instant. He might well remember him, for he had been one of Robin Hood's unwilling guests, and had paid for his meal with a good deal of money he had had in his saddle-bag. So the instant he felt sure that Robin it was, he slipped out from the church, and sent a message to the Sheriff and his men that Robin was in the church, and they had better come and take him.

With all speed the Sheriff made haste, and even as Robin knelt in the church itself, he heard the tramp of many feet, and saw himself surrounded. It was a hopeless case, Robin was unarmed, he had none of his men with him, and the Sheriff's men were not a few. He made

for the crowd, as though he were armed, but
they closed in upon him, and though he struggled
manfully he was bound hand and foot, and
cast into prison. The very next morning the
monk left Nottingham for London to know
what the King desired should be done with
the man, who, by his express permission, had
been allowed to roam the Forest in freedom
for so many years. Glad at heart was the
monk because of his errand; for at last it
seemed to him he would get level with Robin
Hood.

Meanwhile, the news had reached Little John.
In his heart, as well as that of Robin, anger
had died down. Then when he heard the news
he guessed some messenger would go to the
King from the Sheriff, so he had the roads
watched that the messenger, whoever he might
be, might be stopped. On the road he himself
travelled with another man, in order to reach
Nottingham city, he met the monk, and asked
him concerning his errand, and the monk
boastfully proclaimed that he had been the
means of casting Robin into prison, and was
even now going to London to get the King's
consent to have him hanged.

Little John took care that the monk never

went another step. Then he dressed himself in the monk's garment, and leaving him lying by the wayside, he and his companions went up to London to see the King.

The King never dreamed that it was any but a monk who brought the news to him; for Little John had shaved his head till it was like the head of other monks, and he was dressed in the monk's long robe.

So the King made answer: "It is my will that you send Robin Hood to me!" for he thought that to save his life, Robin Hood would swear to enter his own service once more, and that all Robin's skilled archers would swear likewise so as to save their master.

The very next day Little John departed with a letter from the King with a great red seal. But on the way he bought some fine clothes to dress himself and his man fittingly, as though he were a real messenger from the King. Thus it was that when they arrived in Nottingham at the house of the Sheriff, that good man was completely deceived, and so was his bitter-tongued wife.

They feasted them both as though they were the King himself, and the Sheriff ate and drank until he grew sleepy, and Little John and his companion pretended to do the same.

The Sheriff's wife left them together to sleep off the effect of their heavy meal; but as soon

as the Sheriff was snoring deeply they both got to their feet, took down the keys of the gaol from where the Sheriff kept them on the wall, and made straight for the prison itself, and set Robin free.

The days had gone by so slowly, and there seemed so many of them, that Robin had lost hope. They had passed into a week, and the week had become ten days, and this was the eleventh! Never a word had Robin heard from his own Merry Men, and he could only conclude that Little John had told them of his quarrel, and they had all taken Little John's part, and that was why they had left him to his fate. That was why, when he saw them, his heart grew as light as that of a schoolboy: and it was not because they had come to set him free, but because he saw they loved him still.

Once Robin was free they crept out of the gaol behind the Sheriff's house, and stole by back ways through the town itself to where it was easiest to climb the wall. Little John let his companion climb on to his shoulders, and then Robin swarmed up over the other two till he rested on the top of the wall. Then he gripped with his hands a rope ladder Little John had brought with him, and as Robin held the top of it with all his strength, the other two mounted as quickly as they could. Then they held the ladder, and Robin descended on the other side. Little John then took hold of the rope ladder and his companion climbed

down. Once he was below he stood on the
shoulders of Robin Hood, and Little John,
throwing the ladder down, clung on to the top
of the wall until his feet rested on the shoulders

of the top man of the two, and he very quickly
let himself slip down hand over hand over
them.

Away the three rushed: but all during the
long journey to the old camp under the green-

wood, there was very little said. Both Robin
and Little John remembered their quarrel, and
Little John was too proud to make the first
advances. But as they drew near to the camp
itself, Little John suddenly pulled up, and said,
sternly:

"I have shown you, Robin Hood, that I
held no malice in my heart for the blow
thou gavest me. But a blow it was and Little
John takes blows from no man, not even from
thee. What I said, I stick to. Thou art no
more master of mine, and I am no longer
thy man."

He was striding away with his head held up
proudly, when Robin called him back.

"This shall never be!" said Robin stoutly.
"If thou wilt not be man of mine any longer,
I will be *thy* man. I make thee Chief of our
band upon the spot, and I will serve thee as
thou didst serve me."

"Nay," answered Little John. "That shall
never be! If we serve, we serve together as of
old." And he held out his hand, saying:
"Comrades, or nothing!"

Then Robin gripped his hand, and answered
with all his heart in his voice:

"Comrades, let it be!"

So Little John rescued Robin Hood, and when the King heard of the trick which had been played him, he cried:

"Would I had to serve me, such men as Robin Hood has to serve him!"

THE DEATH OF ROBIN HOOD

You have lived many years with Robin Hood, "under the greenwood tree," as you have read or heard these tales. You have seen him come and go with his Merry Men, always in danger, always running risks! A bold man, none more brave; a kind man, none more tender-hearted! And more than all else, an independent man who took his own way in spite of Sheriff, Abbot, or King

This free and easy life of his with his Merry Men went on for many, many years: but no matter how strong a man may be, nor how independent, there comes a time when he has, yes, simply HAS to rely upon others instead of himself! Everyone, sooner or later, falls ill, and when that is the case, the proudest and most self-willed of us all has to be nursed and tended by others. Not even Robin Hood could escape!

For many years he had had simply wonderful

health. Never a pain, never a cold! But one day Robin Hood felt very strange. He got up to breakfast, and it was set before him, but he merely looked at it, he could neither eat nor drink. Thinking the trouble would pass off, he took his bow and arrows and went out for the purpose of shooting with Little John, but they had not gone far into the Forest when Robin suddenly turned dizzy, and fell down on the heather and the bracken, while Little John stood looking at him with dismay. What did it mean? What could it mean?

It was a long time before Robin opened his eyes at all, a very long time, and even then he did not seem quite to know where he was. But at last he seemed to take in that it was Little John looking at him, looking at him with very anxious eyes.

"Master," he said, "methinks thou art going to be ill. Perhaps very ill!"

Robin smiled wearily, and as he struggled to get up, he said: "Methinks thou art right! It is a strange thing that amongst all the men in our Merry band we have no leech. But never have I missed his presence until this morn. I must bethink me what must be done!"

So Little John helped him back to the camp, and very quickly the news spread amongst the Merry Men that Robin Hood was ill, yes, very ill.

Robin lay there dozing, seeming half awake and half asleep, and taking no notice of his surroundings. To tell the truth, he was dreaming. There kept coming before his eyes the scenes of his childhood. How he had ridden with his mother to Squire Gamwell's, at Great Gamwell Hall, Nottingham. Ah, his mother had gone now! He remembered how the riot had occurred, which caused him to be seized by the Sheriff, and how he had escaped the Sheriff's officers and come into the Forest. He remembered his father and the way he brought him up so well. But while he remembered these early scenes, there suddenly appeared the face of a cousin of his, a girl who had become a nun, and during the years, the many years in which he had been living his free and open life in the Forest, had shut herself up in a nunnery near Nottingham, and as the years went by had become the Lady Abbess of the place. He had never thought of her for years, but he did so now; for in those days most of the nuns were quite skilled at nursing and in treating people who were sick.

So, presently, he turned over his head towards Little John, who saw there the very picture of despair, and he said to him: "I have a cousin who is the Prioress of Kirke Hall Abbey, near Nottingham. If thou and the men canst carry me thither, she will nurse me for old time's sake, and make me well."

So they made a litter and slung it upon poles, which they carried on the shoulders of four brawny yeomen, and they set off towards Kirke Hall Abbey.

It was midday when they started. It was drawing towards early evening when they reached the postern door of the Abbey, and set the bell clanging.

The porteress opened the gate, and when she heard what they had to say she went back into the Abbey and told the news to the Abbess.

"What!" cried that good lady. "That scamp! That rascal who has robbed so many a holy monk and even the Abbot himself. I will go down to him!"

In a minute or two that lady made her appearance, and Little John noticed that as she looked at the cousin she had not seen for so many years, a curious gleam came into her eyes of something which appeared like spite and malice.

The look disappeared instantly, and its place was taken by the smile of pleasure with which she welcomed the men.

"Ye must bring my cousin in, and lay him down in a room which I will show ye," she said. And, obediently, they lifted Robin Hood up, and carried him in.

"Now," she said, "ye can go away with an easy mind. Your leader has but a touch of the fever, and I will simply bleed him, and he will soon get well."

So they departed, leaving their master, who had been so independent all his days, lying there helpless in the hands of these women.

It was easy to tell them to go away, but Little John felt so worried and uncomfortable that he did not go far. He could not forget that sudden gleam in the eyes of the Lady Abbess; and, suddenly, while he was thinking hard about it, it came to him quite clearly that the Lady Abbess would be sure to put what she would consider the evils Robin had

done to the Church in the district of Nottingham
before any feeling she had for him as her cousin.
Supposing, just supposing this woman took
advantage of his helplessness to have him

seized while he was there; or allowed him to
die through neglect. The thought so startled
him that after he had been gone about an
hour, he crept back to the walls of the Abbey
and listened.

It was well he did, for presently, very, very faintly, he heard three tiny blasts on Robin Hood's bugle horn. The very faintness of the sound convinced him that something was wrong, so springing up he climbed over the walls of the Abbey, broke into the grounds, strode into the building, and made his way upwards, till he reached the room where Robin Hood lay.

Ah, it was just as he thought. The wicked woman had opened a vein, as doctors always did in those days, and then she had gone away and left the man whom she considered the enemy of the Churches to die.

Little John bound up the vein tightly, and sat there to mount guard.

Robin Hood, however, grew weaker and weaker, and presently he said:

"Little John, I am finishing. Something tells me I am too weak to rally. But give me once more my bow in my hand, and let me send an arrow through the window. It will be my last."

Little John raised his master and carried him to the window, and with one final effort, Robin sent his last arrow speeding through the casement. All his great strength seemed to

come back to him for that one shot, and when
he had sped the arrow thus, he fell back,
saying:

"That was a long shot, Little John. Over
the walls of the Abbey it sped, and far into

the Forest. When you have laid me down,
and I am gone, go, search for that arrow, and
where thou dost find it, there bury me beneath
the sward!"

Late that night the soul of Robin Hood passed away. They buried him, as he had asked, just where they found the arrow which he had shot. But they never could bury his memory.

Somehow, as the years came and went, the people who had grown up at their mothers' knees in Nottingham district, told their children in turn when they came; and never fairy story pleased the bairns so well as this old tale of Robin Hood.

"The years flew on:—the years flew fast.
　　Those who had lived near Robin's day
Seemed people of the Long, Long Past.
　　But tales of Robin's life and way
Were tales that ever seemed to last.
　　　　This tale of Robin Hood!

A hundred years and more had sped;
　　Five hundred more had told their tale.
Much more there was that could be said,
　　Of field and forest, hill and dale.
But still old Robin's story led:
　　　　This tale of Robin Hood!

Then came our fathers' time and day,
　　When books no longer were a few,
They read of Drake and Nelson's way,
　　Of those whose stories were quite new.
But still old Robin held his sway,
　　　　In tales of Robin Hood!

And, still, wherever children meet
  And ask for stories to be told,
Parents still feel that nought can beat,
  This tale of Robin Hood of old.
And so this tale we still repeat,
    This tale of Robin Hood!"

THE END